Praise for *They All Said Amen*

Like a jeweler exposing the depth of beauty hidden within a diamond, Patricia Marks' deceptively simple stories open up facets present within the New Testament but rarely mined with such insight. Her stories from unheard voices are filled with allusions that reveal these fecund stories to be deeply biblical. We experience Lydia's baptism in Acts, for example, and the transformation as she comes to know the Christ who understands toil, hunger, and betrayal. With the cleverness of Rahab and the courage of Deborah, these stories bring out treasure new and old from familiar passages. They leave the reader with much to reflect on and a hunger for more.

The Rt. Rev. Frank Sullivan Logue
Bishop of Georgia

Each and every short story in this book is a gem—and like any gem, the more you gaze at it, and turn it over in your hand and gaze even more, the more beauty you will see. Each of these stories about people often overlooked in the Bible is beautiful and evocative, replete with memorable images of grace and love that will immediately resonate with readers, especially those who themselves may feel overlooked. You cannot read this book without feeling lifted up. I highly recommend it."

The Rev. Dr. Dave Johnson
Rector, Christ Episcopal Church
Valdosta, Georgia

My dear sister in Christ, you have blessed me for asking me to review your sample stories. I have read these passages before but never thought to put the human side to it, the people that made these stores for us to read and come to love. I could not stop reading them. I have read them several times, enjoying them more and more. I loved each and every story, and I am looking forward to reading the rest of "They all said Amen." I highly recommend this book to everyone who would like to see how that passage actually came to pass from the person it actually happened to. I would give it 5 stars.

Archdeacon Yvette Owens
Diocese of Georgia

In this book we meet a distraught mother seeking to save the life of her sick daughter; a young man giving thanks for his freedom from an illness; a man finding purpose and direction after the loss of his identity. These, and many others, give witness to the power and presence of God in the lives of many. In the lives that we read of here the writer, The Reverend Patricia Marks, has reflected on her history and experience as a Deacon of the church and on the lives of many she has served. She has gone beyond words to give us a picture of lives of faith. Here is a book that speaks of compassion and understanding for all.

The Rev. Peter L. Ingeman

The author has a remarkable ability utilizing picture words. This charming instrument allows her to paint stunning images with words by which you will find her writings encapsulating. She takes you on a descriptive journey that is soothing to the soul, mesmerizing, interwoven, and majestic. As she does this so seamlessly, one is reminded of the ultimate expression of love, that of the Cross. Thank you for sharing your visual affect with words; as readers simultaneously gain spiritual inspiration. Hallelujah!

Debra Tann, Ed.D.

"In 'They All Said Amen: Unheard Voices in the Bible," Patricia Marks finds full lives behind brief lines from several biblical passages. She reveals the back stories to people who are briefly mentioned in the Bible but whose stories are important in matters of living and faith. People who encounter Jesus but whose names we often do not know. Dr. Marks creates these stories with insight and compassion, through deep biblical study and profound inspiration. Through her eyes, these stories provide insight not only into biblical passages but for our faith and inspire us in our lives. This is a powerful and beautifully written book.

Dean Poling
Executive Editor, *The Valdosta Daily Times*, and author of the novel *Waiting for Willie*

They All Said Amen

UNHEARD VOICES IN THE BIBLE

Patricia Marks

CrossLink Publishing
RAPID CITY, SD

Marks/CrossLink Publishing
1601 Mt. Rushmore Rd.
Rapid City, SD 57701
www.CrossLinkPublishing.com

Ordering Information:
Quantity sales. Special discounts are available on quantity purchases by corporations, associations, and others. For details, contact the "Special Sales Department" at the address above.

They All Said Amen/Patricia Marks. —1st ed.
ISBN 978-1-63357-348-2
Library of Congress Control Number: 2020942907

*In thanksgiving
for my Christ Church Vespers friends*

.

The Prayer of St. Francis

Lord, make us instruments of your peace. Where there is hatred, let us sow love; where there is injury, pardon; where there is discord, union; where there is doubt, faith; where there is despair, hope; where there is darkness, light; where there is sadness, joy. Grant that we may not so much seek to be consoled as to console; to be understood as to understand; to be loved as to love. For it is in giving that we receive; it is in pardoning that we are pardoned; and it is in dying that we are born to eternal life. *Amen.*

Contents

Acknowledgments

When I was a little girl, sitting on my bedroom floor learning to use a portable typewriter, I decided that I wanted to be a writer. It took many years of academic research and many years of teaching and serving as an Episcopal Deacon—all of which I loved—to prepare the way to retirement, when I can sit in front of a Mac instead of an old Olivetti and plunge into the world of words. I am especially grateful to all those who supported me on the path that led to this collection of stories. I am thankful for the patience, understanding, and wisdom of my Vespers friends who opened both ears and hearts to welcome my homilies, some of which became the basis for the stories in this book. Peter & Happy (my Douglass "sister"), Julius & Julia, and Phyllis & John have dedicated their lives in loving service to others. Monty & Marilyn's creativity, Julie's and Della's friendship, Emily's patience and expertise, Patricia & Jerry's faithfulness—all have served as guiding lights. The Rev. Dr. Dave Johnson has fostered my love of words by inviting me to preach. And this collection is in your hands because of the expertise of the editors at Crosslink, who have welcomed me into the fold.

Without the encouragement of The Rev. Peter L. Ingeman, I would not have become a deacon serving under the gracious leaderships of Bishops Henry Louttit and Scott Benhase, and in retirement under Bishop Frank Logue. Fr. Peter's guidance led me not only to further study but also to an understanding of what it means to be a living bridge between the church and the community.

Above all, I could have done nothing without the loving support of Dennis, my astrophysicist husband and the star of my life, who has made my writing possible by encouraging, proofreading, cooking, providing tech support, and much, much more!

Introduction

"**F**ollow me!"

Now, there's an order—one that puts both joy and fear into the heart of the average listener.

"Follow me!"

What on earth does that mean? Are we, like Peter, called to drop our fishing nets and set off on a challenging road strewn with the rocks of danger and difficulty? What about our families, our jobs, our education? The answer is yes. We *are* called! Look at Luke 9:

> As they were going along the road, someone said to him, "I will follow you wherever you go." And Jesus said to him, "Foxes have holes, and birds of the air have nests; but the Son of Man has nowhere to lay his head." To another he said, "Follow me." But he said, "Lord, first let me go and bury my father." But Jesus said to him, "Let the dead bury their own dead; but as for

you, go and proclaim the kingdom of
God. Another said, "I will follow you,
Lord; but let me first say farewell to
those at my home." Jesus said to him,
"No one who puts a hand to the plow
and looks back is fit for the kingdom
of God." (Luke 9:57–62)

We are called—called to say *Amen* to the invitation to "follow me." But the cost of disciple-
ship is high: it is our whole lives. Many of us may
wonder whether we are strong enough, worthy
enough to follow the Way.

The Good News is, the Way is universal! The
Good News is, anyone, *anyone*, is welcome, no
matter what your position is, no matter where
you have come from. We may stumble, we may
fall, but we are all welcome to take the path that
leads through thick and thin to a glorious awaken-
ing. That openhanded invitation is evident when
you read Bible stories and focus not only on those
who are speaking but on the ones who, like many
of us, are standing in the background, listening.

In the newspapers, at the workplace, in any
gathering, it is those who are in the limelight
whose words and gestures are remembered and
recorded. But the ones who carry the trays of
snacks are there too. The passersby in the hall, the
assistants, are there. We are there too, and we are

listening. Bible stories are like that––they are like real life, with people of all walks of life gathering and events happening.

We have been blessed with a rich bounty in reading the Bible: we have learned how to believe, how to behave, how to help. We have been shown, in short, the path to follow. Yet, we are like those questioners in Luke, yearning to join the Way, but worried about our responsibilities. That is why, in looking at a series of biblical accounts of miracles and events, I have given special consideration to those who are behind the scenes. The disciple's mother, the washerwoman, the curious child, the wedding feast servant—like us, all these and more have been called. I have also tried to imagine how some major figures felt as they tried to pursue their lives after an experience like the one Bars-abbas faced, when he was not chosen to join the band of disciples; or how Ananias felt as he went to see Paul, blinded on the road to Damascus, sitting and waiting for a knock on his door.

My stories, which are based on specific biblical verses, focus on the call to follow Jesus, a call heard by people of all kinds, and followed in a multitude of ways. Ultimately, the stories suggest that even if, like Jesus, you have nowhere to lay your head, you can indeed follow the Way of love and life.

Part One:
Showing the Way

The New Wine of Life

On the third day there was a wedding in Cana of Galilee, and the mother of Jesus was there. Jesus and his disciples had also been invited to the wedding. When the wine gave out, the mother of Jesus said to him, "They have no wine." And Jesus said to her, "Woman, what concern is that to you and to me? My hour has not yet come." His mother said to the servants, "Do whatever he tells you." (John 2:1–5)

The rain came pelting down, turning the narrow paths into muddy streams. Walking back and forth between the wedding tents and the service area, Ami balanced on the slippery pathway, his sandals heavy with water. Despite that, he was thankful to be where he was. His tent was small for the six workers who lived in it, but it was warm, and the food was plain but plentiful.

As he sidestepped a puddle, he thought about how hard his parents had worked. His father had labored in the fields, and his mother mended clothing when she wasn't minding all his brothers and sisters. He remembered growing up in tents with patches, little kindling to keep the fire going, and less food. Now, he was fortunate to be a part of a wealthy family—well, not a real member, but at least valued enough as a servant to be taken care of.

His thoughts turned to the wedding party he was helping to set up. Since the groom was the eldest son, guests were coming from far and wide, some even from Galilee, where the well-known carpenter named Joseph lived. It was Joseph who had journeyed to build the add-on to the family's house so that the groom and his bride would have a comfortable place to start a family.

Reaching the shed, he hefted another bag of figs to his shoulder. He sighed as he thought that he, too, would like to have a family of his own. A son! Maybe he could find a way to build a new life, he thought, as he pulled up his hood and trudged back out into the rain.

"Ohhh!" He heard a sudden wail and then the sound of sobbing.

There at his feet was a young girl, the tears on her face mingling with the rain. She had slipped and fallen, and the tray she was carrying loaded with soup cups had landed in a mud puddle.

"They are broken; they are broken. They will cast me out. Oh, what shall I do!"

Ami put the figs down under the shelter of a doorway and ran back to her. "Child, child," he said soothingly. "Aare you all right?"

She looked up at him, her long eyelashes wet with tears, and he realized with a jolt that this was no child. It was the face he had dreamed of, the one he had been seeking to make his life complete. He took a deep breath and said, "What is your name?"

"Shiprah," she answered, wiping her eyes.

"Beautiful, just like her name," he murmured to himself and drew her up out of the mud. "The cups are fine, just dirty," he said soothingly. "Come, let us wash them, and all will be well."

As quickly as they could, they put everything in order and went to the cooking tent, where they heard a commotion.

The wine steward was complaining loudly. "There is no more wine! We have run dry! This crowd—I've never seen anything like it." He wiped his brow. "Wine and more wine, that's all they want."

At that, the woman named Mary, who had been inspecting the food trays, threw her hands up in the air. "No more wine?" she said in dismay. "It's an omen. It can't be—that honorable couple—all they have will be taken away." She turned to a young man who was standing quietly with four of his friends. "Do something!" she demanded.

He looked at her and said with a trace of sadness in his voice, "Mother, mother, why should it matter to us? All will be taken away, and all will be given."

Turning his gaze to Ami, he said softly, "All will be given." Ami, who felt a shiver down his back, reached out and pulled Shiphrah closer.

He smiled at them and said, "Be patient. Your hour is coming." He added quietly to himself, "And so is mine." Then he pointed at a row of tall stone jugs. "Fill those with water," he commanded.

Ami gestured to the other servants, and together they trudged back and forth to the well until the jugs were full.

Some of the guests, curious about the delay, had gathered around. "Are we doing the rite of purification?" some asked. "This is a celebration, not a burial!" others complained. "Maybe it's the bride," another said, skeptically. "She must be purified, or she cannot have sons."

Jesus shook his head. "They will find that there is another kind of purification," he murmured to himself. Then he intoned, "Let the chief steward taste." And Ami, who had been wondering at the fragrance rising from the water jars, leaped up, took a water scoop, and filled a flask with blood-red wine.

The crowd fell silent, and he stood rooted to the ground, scarcely believing what he saw. Then, with shaking hands, he carried what had been water to the chief steward who tasted it and stared at Ami in amazement.

"Where did this come from?!" he said. Walking over to the bridegroom, the steward handed him the flask. "We have found more wine," he said, bowing formally, and then, with the intention of gently reminding the newly-wedded host about serving etiquette, whispered to him, "Everyone serves the good wine first, and then the inferior wine after everyone is drunk. But you have kept the good wine until now!"

The bridegroom took a sip, and his eyes widened. "Let the celebration continue!" he shouted joyously.

After a moment of stunned silence, Ami walked back to where Shiphrah was standing. As he approached, she blushed and bent her head. "Come, little one," he said. "Let us serve the guests. And then, my sister has made some soup, and we too shall eat." He held out his hand, and timidly she took it.

They turned and found themselves face to face with Jesus and his mother, who were gathering their belongings. Mary's tears had dried, and she was smiling. "They did what he asked," she said proudly. "My child is a boy no longer. He is a man, and he will climb to great heights."

Pulling Shiphrah down with him, Ami fell on his knees and kissed the hem of Jesus' robe.

"What can I do for you?" said the voice above him.

Ami was silent, and then the words came. "If you can make wine out of water, O Great One," he ventured, "then what can you make of us?"

The man softly chuckled and bent over them, laying his hands on both of their heads.

"It has already happened," he answered, "Ami, you transform what you touch with loving-kindness."

As Ami raised his head and looked into Jesus' eyes, he could see the bright sun circling his head with a ring of glory.

"You are my servants now, wherever you go, wherever you stay." Jesus turned and called his followers together, set his feet on the western-most road, the one that led to Capernaum.

Ami drew Shiphrah's arm through his as she smiled shyly at him. "You are my beloved now," he whispered, "and I am yours." He wished he had a gift to give her, but that would have to wait. In the background, he could hear the murmur of the wedding guests rise and fall.

"Come," he said. "We have work to do."

Lord, grant us contentment in our daily tasks so that in following the path you have laid down for us, we may serve you all the days of our life. Amen.

The Cave of the Self

They came to the other side of the sea, to the country of the Gerasenes. And when he had stepped out of the boat, immediately a man out of the tombs with an unclean spirit met him. He lived among the tombs; and no one could restrain him any more, even with a chain; for he had often been restrained with shackles and chains, but the chains he wrenched apart, and the shackles he broke in pieces; and no one had the strength to subdue him. (Mark 5:1–13)

I t was dark in those grottoes, so dark that the inky blackness permeated the very dust on the floor, stealthily seeping into the heart and soul of anyone who ventured there. At night the ragged man was lonely beyond measure as he crouched against the wall in fear of the hosts of bygone spirits of those loved by others, those who had no love for him. Nothing kept him company but the pinpoint eyes of some unidentifiable creature whose teeth grew sharper in his imagination as the night progressed.

He huddled there between the tombs, lying on rocky soil with little to cushion his back and less to wrap himself in. And the sores on his wrists and feet, where the guards had bound him with shackles and chains, kept him awake with an incessant reminder of his imprisonment.

"Avar Araphel, Avar Araphel," he howled. In the bleak darkness, he would cry out his own name repeatedly, trying to convince himself that the night would pass, that he himself would cross over to a different place, where the sun shone, and arms welcomed him. For a moment, he imagined he was Elijah, abandoned in a cave on Mt. Horeb, with nothing to eat but the bitter taste of terror. When stones fell—and they did fall like rain sometimes—he remembered all the sharp words he had spoken in the past, the weight of them bowing him to the ground.

When dawn came, he would go out and walk from cave to cave, visiting the tombs, looking for something, he knew not what. His arms were scarred from the boulders and crags that he hurled himself against, looking for an opening into another land. But still, that land remained closed to him, hardened like the hearts of those who had tried to bind him in chains.

He had been too strong for the guards, but this morning the light outside was too strong for him. The sun shone with an intensity that made him stagger; it was brighter than he had ever seen. Then, dimly, a figure appeared before him. It was speaking, softly but distinctly, either to him or something in him—he wasn't sure. Suddenly his whole body tingled, and he felt a rush, unlike anything he had known before. His knees went weak, and he fell down in front of the figure. He heard shouting—something in him was shouting, "What have you to do with me, Jesus, Son of the Most High God?" The words spilled from him without warning. And then all was a blur, and he felt himself writhing and twisting.

He was no prophet; he wasn't Elijah; he just wanted to go back into the darkness and quietness of his cave. "Please, please," he gasped, "I beg of you, do not torment me!"

The man looked at him with pity. "Tell me your name," he said softly. And somewhere, from that part of him, that wasn't really himself, he cried out "Legion! My name is Legion!"

And his real self knew that was wrong, knew that he was really Avar Araphel, the one who wanted to pass through the darkness.

Then the man called Jesus looked up into the heavens and swept open his arms. All at once, everything was in turmoil. Avar's head cleared, and he stood up in amazement. The farmers from surrounding fields were running back and forth, trying to herd their swine, who were twisting and writhing, grunting and growling, and turning wild eyes on one another. Suddenly, without warning, as if they had become joined in body and spirit, the swine ran toward the edge of a precipice and, with a burst of speed, hurled themselves into the water below.

Avar sat back down abruptly. The intense light had faded into the normal light of day, and he became aware that someone was putting a cloak over his shoulders and holding out a pair of sandals. Somewhat dazed, he thrust his feet into the sandals and, looking up, found one of Jesus' companions holding out a staff and a hat to shade his face.

He became aware of a growing clamor behind him. Word had spread, and people came running from all directions.

"What am I to do—you have killed my animals! They were ready to go to market." The crowd grew louder and louder. "That man is dangerous! He came from the tomb where the madman lives!" Some picked up stones as they came close to the cave.

Jesus looked at them and shook his head. He said softly, "I bring life from the tombs, and I stand with those who are hated and reviled." He started to walk toward his boat, where his companions were standing. Then he turned to Avar. "Rejoice," he said. "You will receive your reward."

"Please," Avar said haltingly, "please. Let me come with you—that would be my reward."

Jesus paused and shook his head. "You have a new life now," he said. "You have passed through the land of darkness into the land of light; now, you must return home and show others the way."

Avar bowed silently. Looking into his own heart, he was amazed to see that the demonic darkness that had plagued him for so long had vanished. In its place was the shining image of the woman he had married and the children they had raised. He knew Jesus was right, and he was filled with longing.

Avar set his shoulders resolutely, grasped his staff, and turned his back to the tombs. He was crossing over to a different place, one where the sun shone, and arms were open to welcome him. He paused for a moment to look at Jesus, getting into his boat, still taunted by the villagers. He knew people would laugh at him too, that they would not believe what had happened.

As he lingered, he heard a still, small voice say, "What are you doing here? Go and declare how much God has done for you!"

Avar smiled and began his long walk home.

Dear God, may we be freed from the demons that hide your face from us. Grant that we may carry your grace and mercy to all those we meet. Amen.

The Gift of the Kingdom

The Lord appointed seventy others and sent them on ahead of him in pairs to every town and place where he himself intended to go. He said to them, "The harvest is plentiful, but the laborers are few; therefore ask the Lord of the harvest to send out laborers into his harvest. Go on your way. See, I am sending you out like lambs into the midst of wolves. Carry no purse, no bag, no sandals; and greet no one on the road. Whatever house you enter, first say, 'Peace to this house!' And if anyone is there who shares in peace, your peace will rest on that person; but if not, it will return to you. . . .Whoever listens to you listens to me, and whoever rejects you rejects me, and whoever rejects me rejects the one who sent me." (Luke 10:1–11, 16)

A young man with curly red hair stood at the edge of the crowd, carrying a small parcel filled with bread and cheese and olives. "Stay strong, Yirmaya," his wife had said, handing it to him. Tears were in his eyes as he embraced her, vowing to return and bring her a gift worthy of the love they shared. Now he struggled to turn his attention to the Leader, who was sending them off into the unknown.

He looked at his feet as the Leader told them to go on their way, just as they were. "Take no extra sandals?" he thought. "Who has extra sandals?" His own were worn to threads, and his feet were caked with the sand of the ground. He knew that before long, he'd be walking barefoot.

His friends were restless, ready to go. Several women sat quietly on the side, weeping, their children gathered close by. Others—a different kind, Yirmaya thought, moving unobtrusively away— others were weaving through the crowd, hovering close to the men they hoped to accompany.

"Shake the dust off our feet?" he heard one of the men growl. "I'll shake more than that if someone won't give us shelter."

"No, no, that's not the idea," another answered. "We're bringing *them* a gift—the villagers are supposed to treat us like royalty."

"Then why are we traveling without helpers, with no bags and no robes?" asked a third.

Yirmaya shook his head. Somehow, he didn't see it that way. He thought they were more like servants of the one who sent them; they were *his* helpers, hardly worthy to carry the gift he gave them. They were supposed to bring peace, and somehow, they were to speak in Jesus' voice. It was confusing, but one thing was for sure—they were to travel like ordinary people, not kings. Yirmaya knew he would need a great deal of courage to speak to strangers, especially those who might kill you for what you were saying.

He sighed and ran to catch up to where his friends were quietly conversing.

"This is a heavy burden," Mordecai was saying. "It's as if he poured all his words into us, and now, we have to say them."

His friend Omri nodded in agreement. "And they are such beautiful words. But I can't remember them exactly."

"That's all right," his brother chimed in. "We have to tell his story in our own way."

With that, the four of them laid hands on each other, bowed their heads, and stood silent for a moment. Then they squared their shoulders and set foot on the path.

They spent that night under the stars, lying on a grassy slope. Yirmaya's family had been poor, so he was used to making do. Before he pulled his cloak over his head, he looked around. *So much beauty*, he thought, *and I deserve so little of it*. Nearby there was a small hole in the ground where some creature—probably a mole—had burrowed.

"Wish I could do that," one of his friends laughed. "Then I'd have a safe place to lay my head."

The next morning, they gathered in a circle and whispered words of thanks for the new day. After they shared the little feast Yirmaya's wife had prepared, they looked around and saw some lodgings near the top of the hill where they had taken their rest. Omri and his brother waved and continued along the road, while Mordecai and Yirmaya turned and climbed the hill. Before long, they came to a circle of rundown huts some distance away from a beautifully kept mansion with gardens and walkways.

They looked at each other, took a deep breath, and pushed through some overgrown bushes to knock at one of the doors. The wood was splintering, and the doorway matted with dirt and leaves. No one had swept the path for some time.

Suddenly, the door opened a crack. They could see the outline of a slender figure, a face peering out at them.

"Peace to this house!" They said the words together as they had practiced doing it on the road.

Somewhere, from the back, they could hear a man shouting, "Peace! I'll give you peace! There's no peace for beggars in this house!"

The door cracked open wider, and a young boy slipped out. Yirmaya smiled at him. "We ask for shelter in the name of the Lord," he said quietly to the woman, who now stood trembling before him.

The man came nearer. "Don't let them in!" it growled. "This is my house, not yours." The woman cowered back as he shouldered his way past her. "We have nothing, and we give nothing," the man spat at them. "Go your way."

Yirmaya stood his ground. "All we are asking for is shelter in the name of love," he replied mildly.

The man glared at them and slammed the door. They could hear him calling angrily for the boy. "Reuven! Where are you? Come here! It is time to feed the pigs!"

Mordecai and Yirmaya looked sadly at each other and, shaking the dust out of their sandals, started to move on.

Yirmaya felt something tugging at his tunic. It was the boy, his eyes round and inquisitive. He was dressed in rags, and his shoulder looked bruised as if someone had grabbed him too hard. "Please, sir," the boy said.

Yirmaya crouched down and looked at the trembling figure in front of him. "Don't be afraid," he said softly.

"Please, sir," the boy repeated. "You said something about 'love.' But . . ." and he paused as if he couldn't go on.

Yirmaya nodded reassuringly. "Yes," he said, "I did."

"But sir," said the boy, moving closer and looking up at him with wondering eyes, "what is love?"

At that moment, he heard a soft voice. "Please, please, take my boy with you." Yirmaya looked back at the house where the woman stood, her hands clasped in supplication, and tears rolling down her cheeks. Suddenly, there was a hissing noise, and the boy jumped backward. He had just missed stepping on a snake. Without a moment's thought, the disciple reached out and swept the boy up out of danger.

"This is love," said Yirmaya, turning around and pointing at the boy's mother. She ran over to them, and Yirmaya handed the child to her. She gave her son a passionate hug. "Go your way!" she said, thrusting him back into the disciple's arms. "I will love you until the end of time. I have nothing to give you, only a new life."

Yirmaya watched as she stumbled back to the hovel. He thought of his own home. Small, but clean; his beautiful wife waiting to welcome him in the doorway. They had no children, and he had wanted to bring her a gift upon his return.

He settled the boy more comfortably on his shoulders and turned to follow Mordecai along the path.

"Reuven," he said softly to the boy. "You have seen the greatest love of all when a parent gives up a son. But I have good news for you."

The boy looked at him with questioning eyes.

Yirmaya smiled gently at him. "You are my child now."

Father, we thank you for your heartfelt love, which gave us your Son and embraced us as your children. Amen.

Love Breaks Rules

He entered Jericho and was passing through it. A man was there named Zacchaeus; he was a chief tax collector and was rich. He was trying to see who Jesus was, but on account of the crowd he could not, because he was short in stature. So he ran ahead and climbed a sycamore tree to see him, because he was going to pass that way. When Jesus came to the place, he looked up and said to him, "Zacchaeus, hurry and come down; for I must stay at your house today." So he hurried down and was happy to welcome him. (Luke 19:1–6)

Yiskah sat cross-legged on the floor, the cloak she was mending spread out around her. Every so often, she would look up and glance fondly at her son. Myyeh was sitting in front of her, sorting through the pebbles he had collected and carefully arranging them in an intricate pattern.

"*Enge, benge, stupe, stenge,*" he softly chanted as he did so.

He is an intelligent boy, she thought. *Maybe he'll become a fine businessman. Or*, she stopped, considering. *A rabbi! That's it! And he'll need all those counting skills for that.* She sat back, imagining what his life might be like.

Her husband, Zaccheus, wanted his son to follow in his footsteps and become a tax-collector. She smiled ruefully and shook her head, thinking of her son's adventurous spirit. How many times had a friend come and said, "You'd better see to Myyeh—he's out in the field, riding one of my cows!" Once a neighbor hauled him dripping to the door. "He tumbled down the well again! He said he was looking for treasure." Myyeh was a rapscallion, tending to follow his curiosity no matter where it landed him. Now if that could translate into studying . . .

She got up, satisfied he didn't seem to notice his father's absence and left to oversee dinner. After a minute or two, the boy quietly gathered his pebbles and slipped out the door. He knew his father had left to meet someone, and he was curious to see who it was. He headed toward the muffled voices he heard ahead of him, running barefoot through the briars until he tripped and fell. Ignoring the twigs and thorns that matted his hair, he got up and made his way through the multitudes waiting impatiently by the road.

"Oof, what's that?" said a well-dressed man as the boy pushed his way past. "Come here, you little devil!" another exclaimed, rubbing his elbow where the bristles in Myyeh's hair had scraped him.

The crowd was getting restive, craning their necks and climbing boulders to see better.

"He's coming!" someone shouted.

"Who is he?" asked another.

"Oh, just some itinerant," answered the well-dressed man.

"No! His name is Jesus. He's a prophet, and I hear he's a healer," said another.

"Not in my house," replied his companion. "I don't trust these guys who come on foot. Nothing professional about them—no bags, no extra clothes, nothing."

Suddenly, there was a disturbance, and the boy saw a slender man leap up from the crowd to grasp a low-hanging tree branch. He stared, fascinated, as the figure made its way higher to lay full length on a branch overhanging the road.

The boy rubbed his eyes and stared harder at the figure. It was his father! Myyeh knew he'd find him, even though he was so short that he tended to disappear into a crowd—disappear, that is, until his fine, smooth voice would rise authoritatively, and then all would fall silent. The leaves nearly covered his father, and Myyeh moved closer to the trunk, where the shade of the nearby fig tree was a welcome relief from the sun.

That was *his father*, he thought proudly; no one else would have the courage to climb that tree. He looked at it speculatively, his feet itching to do the same.

"Zacchaeus! Zacchaeus!" he suddenly heard. "Come on down!" The stranger had appeared, followed by a large group of his friends. The crowd was parting reluctantly, some reaching out to touch him in the hope of healing.

"We need a place to stay," the visitor went on. "Come down and take us to your house."

Myyeh watched, his heart racing. They were to entertain this man! That would be interesting. Myyeh had heard rumors about him. One of his father's friends, a good man, wealthy and well-respected, someone everyone looked up to because he had kept all the commandments since he was a boy, had asked Jesus, "What must I do to inherit eternal life?" And as the story went, Jesus looked intently at him and said, "Sell everything and give it to the poor. Then, come follow me."

His father's friend had stared in astonishment at Jesus, and then, after several minutes, had turned and walked sadly away.

Word about that encounter had spread from village to village, carried by the field hands who moved from place to place looking for work. The boy shook his head. He didn't really understand—maybe he could ask, once they had all settled down. *Maybe*, he thought suddenly, *I should run and warn my mother that she is going to have company for dinner*! He jumped up, and at that caught his father's eye.

"Come here," Zacchaeus said sternly. "Why are you not at home with your mother?"

Myyeh stood silently, head bowed. He wasn't at home because he liked to go adventuring. He loved meeting new people and learning new things. He loved the feel of dust between his toes.

His father sighed. "Can my son be cured of this?" he asked Jesus. "Can he learn to follow the rules?"

Myyeh shyly looked up at the man, who winked at him and turned to smile at Zacchaeus. "Well, my friend," he said, "like father, like son."

Zacchaeus shook his head ruefully and gesturing to Myyeh to follow, began to lead the way home.

Just then, someone in the crowd, which was growing restive, grumbled aloud. "He has gone to be the guest of one who is a sinner!"

"Unclean, unclean," said another.

Zacchaeus stopped suddenly. "Look at my re-cord," he said. "Joseph! Maoz! Adriel!" He called names into the crowd. "Have I defrauded any of you? Bring proof," he said, "and I will pay you back four times over."

He looked around, and the crowd grew silent. No one stepped forward. As they started to move, Jesus' eyes fell on a family of beggars crouched by the wall. Their faces were thin, and their hands outstretched in pleading. A young, ragged girl was cradling a baby, and an older man with a twisted foot tried to stand as they approached.

"I can feed them," Myyeh heard Jesus say softly.

The boy's father stopped suddenly, his eyes filling with tears. "So can I. Half of my posses-sions, I will give to the poor."

Myyeh stood rooted to the ground. Here was his father, a tax-collector, giving up his livelihood. He was like his friend in the story about eternal life. He didn't have to do this; there was no com-mandment that said he had to give away money.

He looked up, questioningly. The tall man crouched down near him and said quietly, "Your father has shown that he loves his neighbor as himself. He has acted on his faith, just as Abraham did so long ago."

Then he stood up and said, "Today, salvation has come to his house because Zacchaeus, too, is a son of Abraham." Then he held his hand out to the boy. "I came to seek and to save the lost," he said. "My feet are on the path that leads us home. Let us go."

And with that, they left the crowds behind as they walked to the house of Zacchaeus, a welcome place on their long path to Jerusalem.

> *Merciful Father, may we answer the call to follow in the footsteps of your Son so that we may learn to walk the path of charity. Amen.*

Crumbs of Faith

She came and knelt before him, saying, "Lord, help me." He answered, "It is not fair to take the children's food and throw it to the dogs." She said, "Yes, Lord, yet even the dogs eat the crumbs that fall from their masters' table." Then Jesus answered her, "Woman, great is your faith! Let it be done for you as you wish." And her daughter was healed instantly. (Matt. 15:21–28)

It must have been hot in the summer, with the sun beating down on the woven goat's hair tent. And then, in the winter, freezing cold, with the fire in the middle, filling the air with smoke and leaving great smudges upon their hands and faces. Or was she wealthier, this Canaanite woman, living in a mud-brick house, the dirt floor covered with bulrushes that grew thick near the river?

Whoever she was, she had spent nights crouched where her daughter lay, nights when this well-loved morsel of flesh and bone tossed and turned, moaning and groaning. Nothing helped, not even the potion of mint, rue, and other herbs she had bartered from the old woman who lived in the woods.

Even the offering she had made to Baal had failed. That was the hardest to bear. She had no possessions of her own, nothing to give to the god, and then, suddenly, there it was, a pearl lying in the dust on the side of the road. She picked it up with trembling hands and ran, heart-bursting, to the old trader, who, muttering and fingering the precious thing, reluctantly counted out only a few coins. With these, she bought a sparrow and carried it to Baal's temple, where the pitiful trickle of blood and feathers was to guarantee her daughter's health.

Running home again, she was sure the girl had been healed—but no, still she lay burning with fever. It was then the mother despaired. This was a girl, after all, and therefore of little value. Holding the tiny bundle in her arms for the first time, she had promised her husband that yes, next time, it would be a boy. But still, she treasured her daughter in her heart, remembering her own mother's words: "The others, they wear their belts broad, and they take the best seats; but we, we make things live. We make good things come out of nothing: we hide the yeast in the dough and make bread; we plant tiny seeds that grow tall and feed our families."

Last night her husband had looked at the child and said with finality, "She is taking all your time. We shall offer her to Astarte; one way or the other, she'll be taken care of." And the mother smoothed her child's hair and knew, as no one cared for the sparrow, not one hair on her girl's head would be saved from that final journey to the temple.

So the next morning, she fed her husband and threw the remainder to the two stray puppies bedded down near the door. After he left, she set out, her dusty skirts swirling around her bare ankles. The women drawing water at the well had gossiped about a new kind of healer. This was her last, her only hope. She knew her husband could put her out for leaving the house without permission, much less for following after a strange man, but she would knock at doors until they opened, she would seek until she found.

It happened suddenly: no trumpets, no red sashes, nothing to distinguish the figure she saw ahead of her. He was walking with such determination that, she thought, he was going to what his kind thought of as the Holy City. A dozen or so men were following him, and as she moved along in the dust, they shook from their every step, she heard snatches of conversation.

Two were talking about fishing; another about walking on or in water, she wasn't sure; and several were arguing about where they would sit when the kingdom arrived—*very confusing*, she thought.

When they caught a glimpse of her, they turned in a body, like a pack of hounds.

"Away! Away!" they cried.

"Unclean," one of them said.

Another sniffed disdainfully and muttered, "Just a woman of the streets."

So she pushed down her fear and shouted over the hubbub, "Lord, Lord! Have mercy on me! My daughter is ill!"

He stopped, very still, and said almost to himself, "I was sent only to the lost sheep of Israel."

When he turned toward her, she felt her knees give way. "Help me, Lord," she whispered, seeing the compassion in his eyes, knowing that this time "Lord" was not just a title but a word of homage.

He stood looking at her, thoughtfully shaking his head. "It is not fair to take the children's food and throw it to the dogs."

One or two of his followers nodded approval at that and began to prod her with their staff to make her move. She looked up, half-blinded by the sun's rays that streamed around him. Thinking of the tiny child she had left behind, something stirred in her. This wasn't Baal, a statue of stone and gold; this was someone who knew what pain was. He wasn't standing near an altar running with blood. He didn't ask for money or for offerings, and he had already broken all rules by speaking to her, giving her a reason for his refusal, almost inviting her to debate.

Out of nowhere, the courage that possessed Deborah, the cleverness that possessed Rahab and Tamar, rose in this nameless woman of no education. Thinking of her own home, she said, "Yes, Lord, yet even the dogs eat the crumbs under the table."

Jesus smiled and stretched out a hand to raise her to her feet. "Woman," he said, "great is your faith! Let it be done for you as you wish."

If she had been Miriam, she would have taken a tambourine and danced home, singing "Sing to the Lord, for he has triumphed gloriously!" But as it was, she kissed the hem of his robe and ran home without stopping to find her child playing in the doorway, laughing at the antics of the two puppies rolling in the mud.

Father of all, we give thanks that your law of love knows no bounds. Amen.

Nicodemus and the Breath of God

Jesus answered, "Very truly, I tell you, no one can enter the kingdom of God without being born of water and Spirit. What is born of the flesh is flesh, and what is born of the Spirit is spirit. Do not be astonished that I said to you, 'You must be born from above.' The wind blows where it chooses, and you hear the sound of it, but you do not know where it comes from or where it goes. So it is with everyone who is born of the Spirit." Nicodemus said to him, "How can these things be?" Jesus answered him, "Are you a teacher of Israel, and yet you do not understand these things?" (John 3:5–10)

Nikos tripped along after his grandfather, stopping to look after a bird that flew into the woods. He wished he had wings, too. He closed his eyes, spread his arms wide, and imagined flying over the stream tumbling down the mountain and soaring into a sky ablaze with the setting sun. Then he turned and raced after his grandfather, who was almost out of sight.

As they climbed, it grew darker and darker, and the boy reached out to cling to Nicodemus's cloak. He could hear the muttered words of a prayer and feel the brambles that had gotten caught on the long fringes. Finally, they reached a clearing where a small fire was burning. There, sitting in silent contemplation in the gathering gloom, was a tall, thin figure, wrapped in a simple red mantle.

Nikos stopped short, and his grandfather bowed so deeply that the seal around his neck touched the ground. "Rabbi," he said.

The man gestured at the ground, and Nicodemus settled a short distance away. "Rabbi," said Nicodemus again, drawing a deep breath, "we know you are a teacher. God must have sent you, for you have done many signs."

He's a teacher, thought the child, *just like my granddad*. He peeked out from behind the cloak where he had hidden. *But he does signs! Granddaddy can't do that*.

Just then, a rush of wind blew some of the glowing embers about. Nikos impulsively reached for one, but the Rabbi shook his head at him.

"No," he said, "it's not the signs that count; it is your own rebirth. You must be born anew, born of the Spirit."

"Look," the Rabbi said, and stood up so that his mantle billowed about him. He seemed to tower over them, covering the earth and sky. "Open your mind, your heart—let the wind blow through you! This is *Ruach*; this is God's breath—when he breathed on the dust of the earth, he breathed the Spirit through us. Do you not know that the word for *spirit* and *wind* is the same?"

Just as Nikos had done earlier, he spread his arms as if he would fly over the whole earth and embrace it, and then, sitting down, became the same quiet figure they had first seen. The child, feeling the wind in his hair, slipped out from under his grandfather's cloak and began to dance with the leaves blown about by the fresh air that poured into the clearing. As he spun around, the thin figure smiled at him, and the boy, overcome by shyness, quickly sat down in back of his grandfather.

The smile faded when Nicodemus asked, "How can this be?"

The Rabbi leaped to his feet and began to pace. "What have you been teaching people, you pharisaical man? You do not understand what happens on earth, yet here is the wind in your face! How can you understand heavenly things?"

He came close to Nicodemus, so close that Nikos could almost feel his breath. "I am doing no signs," he said. "I *am* the sign. I *am* who I am. Forget about the teachings—there aren't 633 ways to worship God! Believe in me—I am *Logos*. It was God's love that birthed me among you."

The wind grew, and the flames leaped higher, flashing and flickering on Nicodemus's face. "You come here at night, in darkness of body, mind, and soul," Jesus said, "but whatever you do, if it is true, must be done in the light. *You* must be the light to other people."

He stared searchingly at Nicodemus, who, after a long moment, rose to his feet, bowed deeply, and walked thoughtfully away. Once outside of the clearing, he stopped and leaned against a tree, bending his head in prayer.

The boy looked back, and on a sudden impulse, ran to the clearing. The embers were still glowing, but no one was there. Off to his right, he saw a shadow standing by the stream. Quietly, he tiptoed down the path until he was close enough to feel the droplets of water bouncing off the rocks.

Jesus opened his eyes and looked thoughtfully down at him. Then he put his hand on Nikos's head. "Go back to your grandfather, my child," he said. "I name you Nuriel, God's fire. We will meet again."

* * * * *

When Nuriel grew old, he often told how his grandfather had confronted the outraged officials at the Feast of the Tabernacles, when Jesus had been teaching in the temple. His children would stare in wonder as Nuriel jumped to his feet and thundered Nicodemus's words: "Does our law judge a man without first giving him a hearing and learning what he does?"

And then Nuriel would sit down and stare into the distance, like the rag-thin figure he had met in the clearing that fateful night. With a catch in his voice, he would tell them about the crucifixion, when Nicodemus, his arms overflowing with myrrh and aloes, had helped Joseph of Arimathea wrap Jesus in linen cloths and lay him with honor in a tomb.

"My grandfather was the best teacher of all," he would say, wiping his eyes. "He himself became a student of the Most High."

> Lord, give us the ears to hear your voice, the eyes to recognize you, and the courage to follow your teachings. Amen.

Walking on Water

Immediately he made the disciples get into the boat and go on ahead to the other side. . . . When evening came, he was there alone, but by this time the boat, battered by the waves, was far from the land, for the wind was against them. And early in the morning he came walking toward them on the sea. But when the disciples saw him walking on the sea, they were terrified, saying, "It is a ghost!" And they cried out in fear. But immediately Jesus spoke to them and said, "Take heart, it is I; do not be afraid." Peter answered him, "Lord, if it is you, command me to come to you on the water." He said, "Come." So Peter got out of the boat, started walking on the water, and came toward Jesus. But when he noticed the strong wind, he became frightened, and beginning to sink, he cried out, "Lord, save me!" (Matt. 14:22–33)

The man lay drenched on the shore, his breath coming in shallow gasps. The fishermen surrounding him stood there helplessly. They had seen this before—a small boat careening into the rocks, a body flying over the bow and vanishing underwater, only to reappear like this man, beyond help.

A small boy crouched near him, his head on the man's chest, his cheeks wet with saltwater and tears. On the other side, his mother rocked to and fro, gripping the man's hand and murmuring, "I will never let you go."

The man's eyelids fluttered. "Adva," he murmured. The boy put his ear close to his mouth, the better to hear. "Adva." He stopped to breathe. "You must be strong. Your mother . . ." he struggled for a moment and gave up. "Fish," he said. "You must take my place. Grow up and be strong and learn to fish." Exhausted, he stopped, and Adva bent even closer.

With his last bit of strength, the man put his arm around his son. "You will be like a fish. The sea is yours. But . . ." he paused for a moment. "You will need to learn to walk on . . ." he broke off and fell back, no longer breathing.

His wife's lament grew louder, and other women came running to help. For Adva, the next days were a blur. People kept coming and going into their tiny house. Food appeared from nowhere, and groups gathered to chant prayers and laments.

He watched much of it from his corner in the main room, barely touching the feast laid out in honor of his father. What was he to do? How could he be strong enough to provide for his mother and his sisters? He looked out the window to where the waves were surging against the shore and shuddered. He had always been afraid of the water. Now, though, it was worse. He never again wanted to feel the tug of the current or the motion of the boat under him. He never again wanted to go outside.

Almost a week later, as he was sitting by the window, watching his neighbors launching their boats, his uncle came to the door.

"Adva," he said in his booming voice, "time to go."

His mother was standing behind him, motioning with her hand. "Get up," she mouthed at him.

Adva rose and walked, head bent, to his uncle. "Come," the man said. "We're going fishing."

The boy never remembered what happened after that. His mother told him that he had looked up and fainted. He was put to bed and not allowed to move for several days. Finally, his appetite got the better of his sorrow, and he slipped out of bed, only to find his uncle and mother in deep conversation.

"Boy," said his uncle, "I'm in need of help. Do you know how to skin a fish?"

Adva nodded. He could do that—as long as he didn't have to go into those waves.

"Good. Then come with me, and we'll get started. You can make some money to help your mother."

Adva could feel his skin tighten. He wanted to shout, "I'll never go out again!" but the thought of his mother and sisters going hungry was too much to bear. So he followed his uncle to where the fishermen came in and unloaded their boats. Skinning fish wasn't what he had imagined he'd be doing, but at least he was helping, at least he was doing part of what his father had said. But he shook his head as his father's words echoed in his ears. "You will need to learn to walk on . . ." Walk on what? The sand? The shore? He still wasn't sure.

One day, as he was sitting in the shade of a boulder quietly skinning the day's catch, he heard a crashing sound and the faint sound of someone calling for help. *Not again*! he thought. A dread fell over him as he saw splinters of wood fly into the air, and a sailor was thrashing about in the water.

And then it struck him. "He's someone's father!" he exclaimed. And almost without thinking, he got up and ran into the water, swimming as he had almost forgotten how to do. Other fishermen were yelling to one another, and a nearby boat pulled up to the drowning man almost as soon as Adva had reached him. He held the man's head above water until the sailors pulled him in and laid him dripping on the bottom of the boat. They were so concerned about the man that they forgot about Adva, so he held on the best he could, treading water as his father had taught him how to do.

As the boat seesawed one way and then another, he caught a glimpse of movement nearby. He nearly lost his grip as he craned his neck to see. It looked as if someone was walking across the waves! Then he saw another boat with a man balancing on its prow. The man paused, then stripped off his clothing, and he, too, took several steps on the water.

Suddenly, he threw up his hands and began to sink. Adva could hear him shouting, "Save me!"

Then Adva felt arms around his shoulders. A sailor had turned, seen the boy, and pulled him out of the water. But Adva couldn't take his eyes off the man who had so trustingly stepped out into the waves.

"He walked on water!" Adva said, pointing.

"No, he didn't walk on water, or we wouldn't have pulled him out," said another, who was still trying to calm the half-drowned man who sat dripping at the bottom of the boat. "Now, you need to help row us home."

Eventually, they reached shore, where helping hands pulled the rescued man out of Adva's boat. The strangers had also landed, and Adva caught sight of the one who had stepped off of the prow. He pushed his way through the crowd, and tugging at his robe, whispered, "Did you really walk on water?"

Peter smiled down at him. "Not by my own strength," he said. "He"—pointing to his companion—"he was the one who called me."

Adva contemplated the figure next to Peter. "Please," he said, "tell me how to do that. If my father had walked on water, he would still be with us."

Jesus bent down and looked intently at him. After a minute, he nodded his head. "Can you swim?"

Adva nodded. "Good!" said Jesus. "That is your way of walking on water. You were given the arms and legs to do so, and you were given the heart to serve others."

He stood up and put his hand on the boy's head. "Follow me, and you will be a fisherman. I will be with you wherever you go."

And for the first time since his father died, Adva smiled. He felt peace in his heart.

God of All Comfort, we pray that you calm our fears so that we may learn to follow in your foot-steps. Amen.

Martha Sees the Light

*When Martha heard that Jesus was com-
ing, she went and met him, while Mary
stayed at home. Martha said to Jesus,
"Lord, if you had been here, my brother would not have died. But even now I
know that God will give you whatever
you ask of him." Jesus said to her, "Your
brother will rise again." Martha said to
him, "I know that he will rise again in
the resurrection on the last day."* (John
11:20–27)

She stood in the doorway, framed by a halo
of smoke that came from the fireplace and
looked at the crowded room. Men were
everywhere—standing against the wall, leaning
on the stone benches that ran the length of the
room, sitting cross-legged on mats, all talking
and eating at once.

She wiped her eyes, already red from much
weeping, and set her jaw resolutely. Then she
turned back to where the women were filling

plates for the hungry guests. She certainly wasn't alone; she just felt that way. All around her were helping hands, hands to give her a hug and hands to prepare the food. All around her was a chorus of voices, urging her to sit down, to rest as her sister was doing.

But Martha was a woman who worked out her grief through her fingertips. The waves of sorrow that flowed through her hands helped smooth the dough for the flatbread, helped slice the fruit and chop the herbs. She wanted everything to be as her brother had wished. She pretended that Lazarus was still there, laughing with his friends, telling stories, discussing village matters—that made it easier for her to lay out the funeral spread.

She had called for the lamb to be slaughtered, and the fragrant scent of the stew filled the house. Laced with onions and garlic, sprinkled with a handful of cumin seeds, and spiced with coriander, it was her brother's favorite dish. Last year's dried fish, hardly enough to feed a family, much less the funeral crowd, had been soaked and mixed with broth and tiny balls of meal, and it overflowed the pot where her neighbor's wife was ladling it into bowl after bowl.

She heaped dried figs and dates around a mound of soft cheese and carried it into the room. It was then that she heard someone say, "He is coming!"

Martha nearly dropped the tray. "I heard he was seen near the tomb," another answered.

She carefully put the tray down in the middle of the room and left without saying a word. No one followed; they were absorbed by the food. In any case, they were so used to her taking care of sudden emergencies, unexpected tasks that her quick movements went unnoticed.

She left the house and ran up the small hill toward the thin figure that stood illumined by the sun. *I would pour oil over his feet*, Martha thought, *but it has all gone to anoint my dear brother*. With that, grief overwhelmed her, and she fell to her knees.

"Why, oh, why have you forsaken us!" Martha wept. "My brother would not have died, had you been here."

As she looked up at Jesus, half-blinded by tears, she saw him silhouetted against the fig tree her brother had planted, now beginning to bud. His companions were silent, their heads bowed. Jesus reached down and touched her forehead, and she felt a quiet warmth spread in her heart, a sense that finally, she was no longer alone.

Suddenly, she sprang to her feet. Her sister needed to be here—Mary would be devastated at the thought she had been left behind.

So Martha ran quickly back to the house, woke Mary from her nap, and breathlessly told her that

Jesus had come. On their way to the tomb, as they wove their way through the gathering crowd, Martha saw some faces that were sharp and knowing, twisted and critical. She heard voices she didn't recognize, grumbling under their breath.

"He's going to try to do a miracle," one sneered.

"Maybe he'll succeed," said another, doubtfully.

"It's on our heads if he does," replied a third. "There will be a rebellion, then the legions will come—and that's the end of all of us."

Martha was gripped with fear. They were hoping her brother's friend would fail. She could feel it! *They were ready*, she thought, *to surround him and carry him off. Surely the Almighty would not allow such a thing*, she thought. Surely, if Jesus really was what he said, he would not have to die!

She heard him praying near the tomb and hurried to catch up. "Lazarus, come out!" he called.

It was still. So still.

Then they heard a faint rustle as if someone were stirring.

And Lazarus walked out of the tomb.

After a moment of stunned silence, everyone began to speak at once. Jesus raised his hand to stop them as they surged forward. "You are freed from death," he said to Lazarus. Then he gestured to his disciples. "Take off his grave clothes and let him go."

Those who accompanied Jesus hung back, all but Thomas, who moved hesitantly forward and stretched out a wondering hand to touch the newly risen Lazarus. At that, a great hubbub arose, and eager hands reached to unwind the wrappings.

Mary, overcome with joy, fell at Jesus' feet.

But Martha, who had watched a group of disappointed and angry men slip silently away, walked thoughtfully down the hill and into the house. She wanted to stay, to join the crowd of joyful celebrants, but she had work to do. Her brother's room needed cleaning, and there were dishes to wash and dinner to make for those who returned home with him. And afterward? Jesus would be on his way, walking to Jerusalem.

She stood a bit straighter. Her sister Mary was innocent and childlike, and Lazarus needed rest. Her own path was clear, lit end to end with a shining light.

Spirit of Truth, may we, like Martha, be faithful witnesses to your works of redemption. Amen.

The Cloak of Redemption

Then they brought the colt to Jesus and threw their cloaks on it; and he sat on it. Many people spread their cloaks on the road, and others spread leafy branches that they had cut in the fields. Then those who went ahead and those who followed were shouting, "Hosanna! Blessed is the one who comes in the name of the Lord! Blessed is the coming king- dom of our ancestor David! Hosanna in the highest heaven!" (Mark 11:7–10)

He had a shock of brown, unruly hair, this boy, the one who stands in the midst of the crowd. If you look into his eyes, you see depths upon depths, like pools of deep water, and around the edges, some movement, some perturbation, as if someone had thrown stones into a pond. He had a thoughtful face, and he was thinner than most boys his age. There was a frail air about him.

Yet he waits quietly enough, one of many gathered at the crossroads. There are mothers holding hungry babies; grown men ill-equipped for anything but fieldwork, jeopardizing their hard-won jobs by their very presence. Teenagers, old beyond their years at thirteen and fourteen, scrambling and jockeying to see the Hope of the Future. And the elderly, leaning on sticks cut from trees, crouching near the front, weary with waiting but determined. Near the back, several well-dressed men linger nervously, their silken robes glinting in the shafts of sunlight. They look uncomfortable but resolute.

The boy stood quietly, but it was not always so. Throughout his childhood, he would feel something come over him, and sometime later— he could never tell how long—he would awaken, covered with the dirt and dust of the ground where he had fallen, his sisters gathered around him holding up their shawls and spreading their skirts to protect him from the curious stares of the villagers. Later, they would tell him how he had writhed and twisted and clenched his teeth, but he never remembered that.

Always it was like coming back from the dead; always it was as if he had entered a new world, his senses sharpened, his ears hearing and eyes seeing what others couldn't perceive. His parents, laborers like all the rest, refused to let him work, frightened that one day he would fall into water or fire or be left behind in the fields. All that, until . . .

Until his father, with love for his son shining in his face, had gone to a rabbi, a teacher, and had asked for healing. What courage that took, his son marveled; what courage, for a meek and reticent man, to brave the ones he worked for, to brave the wrath of the leaders, to set himself up as a laughingstock. His father had told the story again and again, how he had pushed through the crowds surrounding the teacher who had just come down from a mountain with some of his followers.

"Rabbi," he had said, "please cure my son! Whenever the spirit seizes him, it dashes him down, and he foams and grinds his teeth and becomes rigid." What honesty, what love it took for his father to say, "Teacher, I believe in you; help my unbelief!"

At that, the teacher, shaking his head impatiently at the murmuring crowd, had taken the boy by the hand and lifted him up. Ever since then, he had been at peace, spending every spare moment sitting at the feet of an old man in the village, learning all he could about the one who had granted him life. Still, every so often, his senses would suddenly sharpen, and his eyesight change and people were afraid of what he would say, for it seemed he looked right through them into the truth of their hearts.

Now, peering between the people in front of him, he sees a colt come slowly down the road, the man on it almost too tall, his feet nearly touching the ground. As it approaches, the crowd becomes noisier and noisier, and the boy's head begins to throb in the old, familiar way.

"Hosanna!" everyone starts crying. "Blessed is the one who comes in the name of the Lord! Blessed is the coming kingdom of our ancestor David! Hosanna!"

At that, the boy looks more closely, and his heart swells with joy. It is the teacher who took pity on him, pity on his father. And he too tries to cry out, with the rest, but cannot. "Save us, deliver us!" That is what the boy's father begged of the teacher. He remembers, as if in a dream, his father falling to his knees in the dust and whispering, "Blessed is he that comes in the name of the Lord!"

"Hosanna! Save us, deliver us!" How many times has Jesus heard that plea? We have run out of wine for the wedding guests—what should we do? My friend, my child, my mother is dying; I cannot see, I cannot hear, I have leprosy, I have a demon. In their need, their desperate need, the crowd cries out for an earthly Messiah, one of the house of David. But they are really crying out for much, much more—for God's grace. For transformation. For God's will to be done.

In that plea for deliverance, we hear the undertone of a memory reaching back to a time when a lamb was sacrificed, and its blood spilled on the doorposts when a whole nation went into exile. That memory is bred in the bone of the One who turns his face resolutely toward Gethsemane, where he himself prays his own version of Hosanna: "Father if you are willing, deliver this cup from me." It is there that his own pure faith speaks in adoration: "Yet not my will, but yours be done."

So the crowd flings their cloaks in front of the colt, lest the mud of the road spatters their deliverer. Old cloaks, torn cloaks, dusty cloaks; cloth with patterns faded and torn; cloaks made painstakingly by hand, handed down, used day in and day out.

Flung without a second thought, these cloaks that sheltered the heads of infants, that covered the backs of laborers, that served as blankets by night. The boy, moved by something indefinable, joins in, pulling from his own shoulders a worn, blue cloak, woven long ago by his mother. The edges are carefully embellished with a tiny pattern, the fringe, lovingly knotted.

As he takes it from his shoulders, he hears his mother gasp, and his father groan. "That is all you have, my son," he says. But the boy is speechless. Eyes shining, he pushes his way to the front and throws his cloak under the hooves of the colt.

What does he see, looking up at the figure who bends down toward him? The dust of the earth shot through with God's own light, heaven and earth coming together in one still point. The old covenant raised up and made new; the poor, the hungry, the grieving made whole; the potential of a new creation springing up in joy.

And the boy, astounded at the greatness of God, falls on his knees in the mud, like his father before him. The boy, possessed by the grace and the love of God, finds his voice and cries aloud, "Hosanna! Blessed is the one who comes in the name of the Lord! Hosanna in the highest heaven!"

> *Lord, give us the courage to dedicate our lives to your Son, so that we may follow him in the cause of truth and for the sake of justice. We pray, especially, that when our time has come, we too may say, "Truly, this is the Son of God." Amen.*

Thomas and the Hand of God

When it was evening on that day, the first day of the week, and the doors of the house where the disciples had met were locked for fear of the Jews, Jesus came and stood among them and said, "Peace be with you." After he said this, he showed them his hands and his side. Then the disciples rejoiced when they saw the Lord. *Jesus said to them again, "Peace be with you. As the Father has sent me, so I send you." When he had said this, he breathed on them and said to them, "Receive the Holy Spirit. If you forgive the sins of any, they are forgiven them; if you retain the sins of any, they are retained." But Thomas (who was called the Twin), one of the twelve, was not with them when Jesus came.* (John 20:19–25)

Eema sat huddled outside the doorway, hands pressed together, and head bowed. She could hear the murmur of voices inside. They were her son's friends—well, some of them were; others found it hard to deal with his questioning nature. He was a bright boy, and his father had taught him to persist, no matter what.

She peeked through the crack in the door and saw the men sitting in a circle, their goblets and plates untouched. She had made them bread earlier that day, hoping that its warmth and scent would bring them comfort. But who could be comforted, she thought, when their friend, their leader, the hope of their life, had been so brutally murdered by the authorities? So there they sat, the fishermen and village folk who had willingly walked away from their everyday lives to follow their mentor, their rabbi, their Messiah. The dust of Galilee still clung to their sandals, the waters of the Jordan still stained their cloaks, and the sound of his voice still rang in their ears.

She sighed. The room was dark, in keeping with their mourning, and in keeping, too, with their safety. She had watched the grieving disciples nail heavy blankets across the windows so that from the outside, the house looked deserted. They all felt their time was near, that those who mistrusted Jesus would be searching for them, too. So Eema had decided she would guard the door. That was the least she could do. Oh, she couldn't keep anyone away; but what she could do was raise an outcry to warn them within.

They were afraid—she knew that, even though these were the ones who had sat with the demoniac in the graveyard. These were the ones who had freely chosen to follow Jesus, from deep in the valleys on up the mountain to be enveloped by God's own presence. They had defied the angry Pharisees; they had been hemmed in and threatened in the Garden at Gethsemane. And now they had locked themselves away. They were frightened not so much of the Romans—whom they expected to be barbaric—but even more so of their own people, the wealthy and educated Jews, the ones whose houses their carpenter sons had repaired, whose clothing their daughters had laundered, the ones who had bought their fish and eaten their produce. *And they should be afraid*, Eema thought: *they are accused of heresy by their fellow Jews and branded as enemies of the state.* Her heart fluttered with fear. Their path—and hers, too—led inexorably toward their own crucifixion.

She leaned closer, listening as the disciples, stunned and grieving, sat mourning for the future of their children born into a world without hope and coping with the knowledge that they were in dreadful personal danger. "My God, my God, why have you forsaken me?" she heard them murmur, echoing the words on the cross.

She closed her eyes, reliving that moment.

"Peace," someone said.

Eema raised her head and peeked into the room. It was filled with light.

"*Shalom Aleichem*," repeated the familiar voice.

It couldn't be, she thought. It was impossible. He had died. He had been entombed.

But there he was.

The disciples were sitting, speechless, their mouths open in amazement.

Their visitor stretched out his hands, still bleeding from the nails. He pulled aside his robe and showed them the spear points etched in his side.

"I am sending you now into the world," he said. "Take with you the gift of the Holy Spirit." Then he breathed deeply on them, held each one of them with his gaze, smiled, and . . . vanished.

Eema collapsed, and the room burst into a hubbub. All she could think of was that her son, Thomas, her son, who needed reassurance, was not there.

That was a week she would never forget. If she had been the only witness, who would have believed her? But all the disciples had seen him! They were all ready to run out and proclaim the good news until a quieter voice or two convinced them to stop and consider what to do next. They did remove the blankets from the windows, and the fresh air and sunlight poured into the room as if it were the first day of creation. *They were freed from the prison of the self*, she thought. Jesus had unbound the cords of despair.

* * * * *

A week later, Thomas rejoined his friends. He was quiet and subdued in the midst of their exuberance. He had been hidden away, he said, but now realized he needed to begin life anew.

"But it's already happened!" they told him. "Jesus was here! Standing right where you are!"

But Thomas shook his head. "How can that be?" he said. "He was crucified. He was buried. How could he stand here like a living person?"

He paced around the room, shaking his head as his friends expostulated. "Why won't you believe us?" one of them finally shouted.

"Unless I see the mark of the nails in his hands and put my finger in the mark of the nails and my hand in his side, I will not believe," Thomas said firmly.

At that, they all fell silent. Then, suddenly, their faces lit up with joy. Thomas, seeing the delight in their eyes, turned.

There was Jesus.

After a moment of silence, he looked intently at Thomas and said, "Put your finger here and see my hands. Reach out your hand and put it in my side. Do not doubt but believe."

Eema saw her son sink to his knees. "My Lord and my God!" he exclaimed.

She opened the door wider, and Jesus momentarily looked her way, a faint smile on his face.

Turning back to Thomas, he asked, "Have you believed because you have seen me? Blessed are those who have not seen and yet have come to believe."

Eema's heart overflowed with thankfulness and awe. It amazed her that Jesus had returned. It was as if he thought it was important for Thomas to understand what had happened. What a marvelous gift! Her son had seen; her son had believed. *It was like an earlier time,* she thought, *when he had asked Jesus how they were to know the way that he was going.* She remembered what Thomas had told her—Jesus had said, "I am the way, the truth, and the life."

Along that way, Thomas had been loyal. He had followed Jesus to Jerusalem, asking the questions that his friends were afraid to phrase. *Without my son, we would know much less,* she thought. Now, she wondered, what gifts could they be giving to others? How could they make others understand the way, the truth, and the life?

She got up, hurriedly from the floor. She would live her life the best she could, she decided, serving those who needed help. *If Jesus could give himself up for all of us*, she thought, *surely, I can reach out even in small ways.*

She headed down the hall to call the other women together. Making dinner seemed ordinary, but they all needed to eat if they were to spread the word.

> *Almighty God, Giver of Strength, may we, like Thomas and the disciples, be so transformed by the power of the Holy Spirit that we turn from our comforts and our fears to carry on Christ's work in the world. Amen.*

Part Two:
Walking the Path

A Heart Known to God: Barsabbas and the Thief's Mother

*"So one of the men who have accompa-
nied us during all the time that the Lord
Jesus went in and out among us ... must
become a witness with us to his resurrection." So they proposed two, Joseph
called Barsabbas, who was also known
as Justus, and Matthias. Then they
prayed and said, "Lord, you know everyone's heart. Show us which one of these
two you have chosen to take the place
in this ministry and apostleship from
which Judas turned aside to go to his
own place." And they cast lots for them,
and the lot fell on Matthias; and he was
added to the eleven apostles.* (Acts 1:15,
21–26)

B arsabbas bowed deeply, one knee touching the good brown earth of Jerusalem. His hands trembled as he traced the sign of the cross in front of him, and he hoped no one could see his face, shadowed by the temple walls.

No one saw him, of course, for all were rushing toward Matthias, wanting to lay hands on him and praying for his strength and courage as the one chosen as the twelfth apostle, the one given by God to replace Judas, the betrayer.

So Barsabbas rose slowly, and putting his hand on the sleeve of the pilgrim in front of him, said a prayer for Matthias, although the words felt stale in his mouth. Had he not walked the path with them from the beginning? Was he not faithful, leaving behind his father's house, his work among the herbs and spices, to take a new name and follow Jesus? He had done his best to help care for the lost and forsaken, the guilty, and the suffering. Why could he not be a chosen witness to the risen Christ?

He knew the casting of lots was final, that the smooth stones with their secret marks were God's own will.

And that was the rub, he thought, as he faded quietly out of the crowd, down a deserted street. That was the rub. He had given all that was in him; and now, in return, he had nothing.

Where was this new path leading him? What was God's will for him?

He thought about the meaning of his name. His mother had died at birth, and his father, who had named him, would say time and time again, "You are Joseph. You will increase all that you touch; you will add to our wealth and double our inheritance."

But he cared little for wealth. He had walked in the same pair of sandals through Galilee, taking no change of clothes with him. And he so loved his Messiah that he even took a new name—Barsabbas, son of the father.

He never thought he would feel so small, so . . . diminished.

So he slipped quietly away, unsure of what to do. Go back home? His thoughts drifted to the laughing dark eyes of his neighbor's daughter. She had been a mere child when he left. Perhaps she had already married, but if not . . .

Suddenly he stumbled against a pile of something. *Rags*, he thought. But no, they were moving, and he bent over the thin form. Her hands were brown and scarred with long years of work, her cheeks were wrinkled, and the wisps of hair escaping from her scarf were grey.

"Come, Mother," he said gently, helping her sit up. "Tell me what is wrong."

She wiped her eyes and looked at him out of the depths of despair. "My son was killed forty days ago," she whispered.

Joseph almost let her fall. It couldn't be. "Are you Mary?" he blurted in disbelief.

She blinked, and her mouth quivered. "I am called Imah Gnieve," she whispered, "the thief's mother. But my heart's name is תֻּגְּכ."

"Your heart's name is Kenut," he repeated. "Honesty."

Rocking back on his heels, he looked thoughtfully at her.

"He was my only son," she wept. "Without him, I have nothing. He fed me and helped me, but only with the coins he earned as a messenger. I wouldn't take from his thievery. And he wouldn't change!" She swallowed hard. "He wouldn't change until the end. Until the very end."

Joseph could almost see the scene—two thieves, one on each side of Jesus, one taunting him and the other asking to be remembered on the day of his death. They were, he decided, like the Urim and Thummim, the casting of lots—one guilty, one made clean.

And then another memory came to mind. One of Jesus' final acts was to create a new family, giving his mother to John and John to her as her son. Here, in front of him, was a helpless woman who had no son.

He had no mother. And here she was.

He looked back at the crowd, their jubilant voices echoing faintly down the corridor. He could just make out the twelve apostles, standing illumined by the last rays of the sun: good men, courageous leaders, all of them. Even Matthias, he thought, envisioning the demanding life the new apostle had ahead of him preaching, teaching, and confronting the authorities at every step.

He turned back to Kenut. Ahead of him, the road was just as dusty as it had been traveling with Jesus, just as difficult. He knew that around every corner he would find the littlest and the least, hungry and thirsty, sick and in prison.

And then, suddenly, a light flashed around him, and his eyes were opened. So that was it! His lot had been cast among his brothers and sisters, and he was to add to their well-being as best he could by living up to both of his names.

With that, his heart leaped up, and he smiled at Kenut. "Come, Mother," he said, helping her to her feet. "We are going home."

> O Lord of the Seekers, help us understand the path that you have laid down for us. Give us the strength and the courage to follow it by reaching out hands

and hearts to those by the way-side. Amen.

Walking, Leaping, Praising: Peter and the Lame Man

One day Peter and John were going up to the temple at the hour of prayer, at three o'clock in the afternoon. And a man lame from birth was being carried in. Peter looked intently at him, as did John, and said, "Look at us." And he fixed his attention on them, expecting to receive something from them. But Peter said, "I have no silver or gold, but what I have I give you; in the name of Jesus Christ of Nazareth, stand up and walk." And he took him by the right hand and raised him up; and immediately his feet and ankles were made strong. Jumping up, he stood and began to walk, and he entered the temple with them, walking and leaping and praising God. (Acts 3:1–8)

The boy Chayim squeezed his way through the crowd and crouched down quietly, his rough brown tunic the color of the dirt under his feet. Next to him, his father nervously twirled a twig up and down, up and down from the fig tree behind him. That was a telltale sign to his son, who rarely if ever saw his father upset. Amidan's large frame was steadily balanced on his ankles, but up and down, up and down went the twig, as if he would lash the well-dressed men gathered by the Beautiful Gate, the entryway to the temple.

The crowd was thick and unusually quiet. The boy looked around, seeing some of his neighbors, who yesterday were so full of joy—yesterday! He himself could hardly believe what had happened. He and his father had been working nonstop at the cobbler shop. Hearing someone come in, they looked up to see his uncle Yaiyr, his arms outstretched, his face shining. His father, putting the finishing touches on the sandals ordered by one of the wealthy landowners, dropped his tools, and slowly stood up, open-mouthed. Yaiyr, who had been lame since birth, was standing on his own two feet! And then they both leaped up and hugged him and twined their arms together and danced. Danced until the dust in the room billowed up around them, until they noticed Yaiyr was barefoot.

"Of course!" they shouted. "Now, you need shoes!" They had laughed until they cried. Neighbors, hearing the joyful noise, had flocked to the door, and together they had all said thanksgiving for the healing.

Today, though, they were quiet and apprehensive. Dispersed among them were others with dour faces, looking suspiciously at their neighbors and listening closely to the slightest comment.

"Silence!"

The sudden clang of a spear handle on the Temple step made the boy jump.

"Shh, Chayim," his father said, drawing his son closer. "It's beginning."

They could see the two strangers walking between guards. They were dressed plainly, almost like his older cousin, who caught fish for a living, the boy thought. But they held their heads up and looked—what had someone called his father? Self-possessed—that was it. *But there was more there*, Chayim thought. Something in the men's demeanor, their fearlessness, their confidence, made him want to go closer.

He knew he ought to stay right where he was. The guards of the High Priest would have no pity on anyone they deemed a danger. Even the crowd of Sadducees, their richly woven robes shining in the sun, would turn on an interloper in a moment. But he counted on the fact that they would overlook him, just as they did when he sidled his way through the crowds to sit by his father.

So when they started to speak, and his father drew himself up rigidly, listening to every word, Chayim quietly slipped away as only a small boy can, threading carefully and slowly through the crowd. He could hear Amidan whisper urgently to him to return, but for one of the few times in his life, he ignored that call.

He found his uncle sitting closer to the front. There, he could hear better, but he still didn't understand. The High Priest was there, as well as Caiaphas and many temple officials he didn't recognize. They were asking about some kind of power that the fishermen had. Chayim thought there was an undercurrent of fear—but weren't they the ones in charge? Perhaps, he decided, the High Priest wanted the power for himself.

The one they called Peter stepped forward. "Why are we being questioned for an act of kindness to a lame man?" He turned and looked at the crowd, his gaze coming to rest first on Yaiyr and then on Chayim. His eyes were large and had a depth that Chayim had never seen.

"It is by the name of Jesus Christ of Nazareth, whom you crucified but whom God raised from the dead that this man stands before you healed," he went on, pointing at Yaiyr. "This Jesus is 'the stone that was rejected by you, the builders; it has become the cornerstone.'"

"Out!" The shout was overwhelming. The leaders, careless of their embroidered robes, were kneeling on the ground to gather stones. Chayim squeezed his uncle's hand. It was cold and trembling. And then suddenly, something happened that astonished him. His uncle leaped to his feet and strode purposely to the front, walking proudly in the beautiful sandals Amidan had given him, the sandals that had been ordered by the landowner.

Chayim jumped to his feet as well. His uncle was walking directly into danger. He was risking his life! The elders were angry, and everyone could see it in their faces. And they were weighing the stones in their hands, ready to throw them.

The crowd grew absolutely silent as Yaiyr took off his sandals, bent down on one knee, and presented them to Peter. His words of conviction rang out for all to hear. "I offer these as a sign and a testimony that I was healed. I give my life for Christ, for there is no other name under heaven by which we must be saved."

"Glory, hallelujah!" shouted the crowd as it surged forward. The guards rushed to meet them, spears at the ready. After one look at the chaos, the officials and elders turned, shook the dust of the earth off their hands and feet, and walked back to the temple.

Chayim ran to the front and knelt next to his uncle. He felt a hand on his shoulder, and looking up, saw in his father's face a mixture of fear and reverence.

Despite the clamor, the shouting, and the pushing and shoving around him, Peter reached down and pulled the boy to his feet. "Walk with your uncle, my child," he said.

"And take your father with you," he added, smiling at them as he turned and vanished into the crowd.

> *Spirit of Christ, we give thanks for the healing power of your word and pray that we may carry your testimony to all those we touch. Amen.*

Ananias, Sapphira, and the Repentant Trickster

After an interval of about three hours Ananias's wife came in, not knowing what had happened. Peter said to her, "Tell me whether you and your husband sold the land for such and such a price." And she said, "Yes, that was the price." Then Peter said to her, "How is it that you have agreed together to put the Spirit of the Lord to the test? Look, the feet of those who have buried your husband are at the door, and they will carry you out." Immediately she fell down at his feet and died. (Acts 5:1–11)

Eliana sighed heavily as she stirred the thin liquid bubbling in the iron pot. It was barely enough to keep them alive, a far cry from her own mother's heartwarming stews, thick with vegetables and meat. Her son Elrad had taken her last coins to the market. He should be back by now . . . and who knew where Casiphia was, she thought angrily, as tears welled up. That husband of hers—what a trickster, leaving her like this. What was she to do? Word was that a group down the road shared food, clothing, everything! She had thought of going to join them, but she had nothing to offer in return.

* * * * *

Casiphia was standing in front of a rug shop, the sun glinting on the gold threads bordering his robe. "This is the chance of a lifetime!" he whispered confidentially to the owner. "All you have to do is—"

Just then, a small boy darted out of the crowd and grabbed his sleeve.

"Hands off!" Casiphia growled, turning angrily. "Elrad! What are you doing here?"

"Father, I have come to the market to bargain," Elrad said staunchly, although trembling inside.

Casiphia looked keenly at him and then patted his head. "That's my boy," he said proudly, and the change in his tone made Elrad smile and stand up straighter. "Tell me, my son, what you have gained."

Elrad held up the parcel of potatoes. "Mother gave me money, and I bought these," he said. "It was a good bargain."

"Aha," said his father. "And what did you do with the remainder?"

Elrad smiled slyly as he had often seen his father do but said nothing.

"I see," the older man said and gathered his robes around him. "Good boy—you will go far. Now leave me. I have business to do." And he winked at Elrad as he turned back to the rug-dealer.

Elrad jingled the coins in his pocket. It was all right, then; his father understood. But his mother? Hoisting the sack to his shoulder, he tried to drown his misgivings by thinking of the juggling games he wanted. He'd save the change he earned this time, and perhaps the next time in the market, he'd make another bargain, and the games would be his.

Arriving home, he threw down the sack and was almost out the door when his mother held out her hand. "The change, Elrad."

He hesitated, the coins growing heavy in his pocket. Suddenly, they heard a shout, then another. "It's the Christians," his mother sighed. "Perhaps they are giving away food."

"No," Elrad said softly, peering out. "Something else is happening."

He stepped out of the house and wriggled under the bushes to see into the field beyond. A crowd of people stood murmuring and pointing at

Ananias, their wealthy neighbor, lying flat on the ground.

"What a liar," the man next to him said. He shook his head and sighed. "He sold his field and kept a portion of the money for himself."

"Why is that wrong?" Elrad put his hand protectively over his pocket.

"Because," the man said, looking at him thoughtfully, " he had promised to give all of his earnings for the common good."

After several men had carried the body away, the crowd dispersed. Elrad, lost in thought, stayed where he was. He hadn't promised to return the money to his mother, but . . .

Anyway, what would she do with it? "Buy ribbons for her hair" is what his father would say. *Juggling blocks were more important than ribbons*, he thought defensively, trying to feel righteous.

But it didn't work, and he was still sitting there when the crowd returned. The same man came and sat by him.

"What's happening now?" Elrad asked.

"That's Peter, our leader. He is rock-steady and honest." Elrad wiggled uncomfortably under the man's observant gaze. "The woman he is talking to is Sapphira, the wife of the man who died this morning."

Elrad could hear her explaining that her husband had sold a field and that yes, the amount he gave Peter was the amount he was paid.

Peter stood up angrily. "That isn't true!" he sputtered. "You are taking food out of the mouths of the hungry. How is it that you both agreed to put the Spirit of the Lord to the test?"

The next moment, a dreadful pallor fell over her, and, like her husband, she fell at Peter's feet.

Elrad felt his heart sink. He had done wrong in keeping the money.

The man next to him looked sideways at the boy and seemed to approve of what he saw. "Come, child," he said. "Take me to your mother. You may have something to give her."

Together, they walked to where Eliana sat sadly, stirring the potatoes into the soup. When they entered, she looked up. "I have brought someone to dinner," Elrad said timidly.

She stood and gestured to the only pillow in the room. "Sit, sir," she said. "We will eat our last supper together."

The man looked at Elrad, and the boy suddenly burst into tears. He heard his father's voice echo faintly in his memory. "Men don't cry! What you have bargained for is yours—yours alone."

But Elrad handed his mother the remaining coins. "Here, Mother. They belong to you."

And then, for the first time in many months, he ran into her arms. As she rocked him and held him close, she looked at the man and whispered, "Thank you. I was needy and wanted my son. You have given him to me." She held out the coins. "Here—take these."

But the man shook his head and gestured toward the door. There was his wife, holding a piece of roasted lamb.

Elrad's mother turned in astonishment. "We have been fed!" she cried joyfully. "We have been fed indeed! Our lives are renewed. Tell us what we are to do."

The man and his wife drew them to their knees. "Pray with us," they said simply.

And great grace was upon them all.

> *O Lord of the Repentant, give us the grace of charitable hearts and open hands and help us be honest through the many temptations of this life. Amen.*

The Heavens Opened: Stephen and the Cloak-Thief

> *"Look," he said, "I see the heavens opened and the Son of Man standing at the right hand of God!" But they covered their ears, and with a loud shout all rushed together against him. Then they dragged him out of the city and began to stone him; and the witnesses laid their coats at the feet of a young man named Saul.* (Acts 7:51–60) – NOT FOUND

"Y ou stiff-necked people, uncircumcised in heart and ears, you are forever opposing the Holy Spirit, just as your ancestors used to do. You are the ones that received the law as ordained by angels, and yet you have not kept it!" The speaker addressed the council with passion and fervor, looking intently at each member as he spoke.

Saul, the young man who stood at the edge of the crowd, was horrified. What a thing to say to the Sanhedrin, to the elders who had studied and prayed, who had been chosen as leaders! He stared, mouth agape at the speaker.

They were of an age, these two, but different. Like Saul, the young man standing in the middle of the court was dressed simply, but his clothing was stained from the soups and meals he had been taking to the widows in the community, and his hands gnarled from all the work he did, from rethatching their houses to digging out their wells. Saul, who was a tent-maker, had worked with his hands as well; but his real love was studying the law, sitting at the feet of the Pharisees, and living and breathing their words.

The crazy apostate went on. "Look," he said, his face alight, "I see the heavens opened and the Son of Man standing at the right hand of God!"

At that, the court erupted. "Blasphemy!" growled Saul under his breath. Everyone there started shouting and covering their ears. But his teachers and mentors did more than that—they grabbed the man, held him aloft, and ran into the field.

Saul nodded in agreement and ran after them. He knew what the penalty for blasphemy was; he knew his teachers had the right to kill this young man. They had cause enough. The heretic had told them that the temple was meaningless—that Y-w-h had no need for a house. Even worse, Saul had heard him say the Holy Spirit transcended the Laws of Moses! Then, if that weren't enough, he had gone on to pretend to see a vision of Jesus standing equally with G-d.

Suddenly, one of the Pharisees, his favorite teacher, turned and beckoned to him. "Here," he ordered, "watch our cloaks for us." And with that, they began to pile their garments around him.

Saul stood proud, happy to help, and delighted to be trusted.

So proud that he didn't see the small figure lurking behind him. He didn't see the thin hand reach out tentatively to caress the thick embroidery on one of the cloaks, the satiny gloss on another. He didn't see the hungry look in his eyes.

The boy Aryeh, who wasn't watching the pursuit, didn't care about fancy arguments about spirit and law or where God lived. What he did care about was finding a way to help feed his family. He patted the coin that hung heavy in his pocket; he couldn't read, but he had felt the outlines of a face—Caesar, was it? The man in front of him had been too incensed watching the trial to feel Aryeh's light touch and agile fingers.

Now, Aryeh thought, *if I can bring home one of these cloaks, my mother will be warm at night, and it is big enough to cover my baby sister too.* So he edged closer and closer, gauging the distance to the trees behind him if he had to run. The beautiful sapphire blue of one of the weavings caught his eye. Saul's attention was riveted on the scene in front of him, and so he didn't see the boy gently slide the cloak from under the pile. Saul didn't move, and the crowd, which was focused on picking up stones, hardly noticed the small figure melt into the bushes with an armful of cloth.

After Aryeh caught his breath, he looked at the intricate embroidery on the cloak and wondered what it would feel like to be one of those men. They had real houses, those people, and servants, and food enough to toss to the dogs.

I could be one of them! he thought. His mother hadn't named him Aryeh for nothing. So he stood up tall and tossed the cloak around his thin shoulders. It covered him completely. He drew the rich fabric up over his face and breathed deeply of the aromatic scent.

And then a strange thing happened.

The sky darkened, and the mocking voices became so loud that he found himself shouting with them. He grew hot and angry and knew if anyone had touched him, he would have acted with murderous rage.

"Aryeh, Aryeh," he heard his mother calling faintly in the background.

He started and threw aside the cloak. He couldn't stop trembling. When he finally felt like himself again, he looked at the cloak with repugnance. He didn't understand what had happened, but somehow he had been transformed by that cloak, and he didn't like it.

I will tear it apart, he thought. *I will make something else of it, something new.*

It was then that he heard Stephen's voice, rising over the clamor and the sound of rocks falling all around him. "Lord Jesus, receive my spirit!"

The crowd quieted suddenly. They were no longer throwing rocks but standing, hands on hips, nodding at one another. And then they began to move away, toward the young man who was guarding the cloaks, pulling their garments from the pile and walking away.

One man, standing empty-handed, angrily began berating him. "Where is my cloak? You scoundrel, you have stolen it!"

"Look!" said Saul defensively, holding out his hands. "I am faithful! I haven't taken anything!"

Aryeh ignored them and creeping closer to the figure lying on the ground, heard the young man cry out, "Lord, do not hold this sin against them." He took a breath and looked directly at the boy, then closed his eyes for the last time.

Aryeh's knees gave way. He knew this man! This was Stephen, the one who brought food to the house when his father had died. This was the one who never forgot to visit, who always shared whatever he had with the children. And now the one who had given them a new life had left his old life behind.

Tears poured down Aryeh's face. He gathered the cloak he was carrying and gently laid it over Stephen's body. As he did, a shadow fell over him.

Looking up, he saw a man with a rock in his hand raised menacingly. "That's my cloak, you fool—how dare you!" he hissed.

Aryeh leaped away as the rock struck the ground next to him. The man pulled the cloak off of Stephen, looking distastefully at the blood and picking off the twigs that clung to the fabric. He strode off angrily, carrying the cloak at arm's length.

At that moment, the sun came out, covering both the boy and Stephen with a warm embrace. Aryeh closed his eyes and turned his face up to the shining source of new hope. And as he did, he thought, *Stephen has a new cloak now.*

> *O Lord of the Repentant, give us the grace of charitable hearts and open hands and help us be honest through the many temptations of this life. Amen.*

The Chosen Instrument: Ananias and Saul

The Lord said to him in a vision, "Ana-nias." He answered, "Here I am, Lord." The Lord said to him, "Get up and go to the street called Straight, and at the house of Judas look for a man of Tar-sus named Saul. At this moment he is praying, and he has seen in a vision a man named Ananias come in and lay his hands on him so that he might regain his sight." (Acts 9:10–12)

Ananias gathered his gifts together, hold-ing the tiny myrrh sapling carefully, its roots wrapped in a piece of cloth torn from his oldest cloak. He balanced a loaf of bread in his other hand and stepped across his door-step on to the Straight Way, the fragrance of the still-warm loaf trailing behind him as he walked.

Suddenly, he felt a tug at his garment. "Karmiel!" he said, looking down at the little, trusting face next to him. "I thought you were with your tutor!"

"Uncle, I am done for today. May I come with you?"

Ananias carefully shifted the plant and put his hand on the boy's head. "How did you guess where I was going?"

He bent down and looked closely at the boy's face. "You love him, don't you?" he said, handing Karmiel the bread. "Come along."

They turned several corners, passing street vendors on the way. Figs and currents and all manner of shawls and woven fabrics were heaped on stands along the street. Ananias nodded and waved off some of the more enthusiastic sellers. "Next time," he said, again and again. "I will be back."

Every few steps, someone stopped him to whisper the news.

"Have you heard about Saul?" said one.

"He is full of anger!" another whispered. "He will bind up anyone who is faithful—even our women! And take them to Jerusalem."

"No, we are safe," a third exulted. "He can no longer see. And maybe he will die! They say he hasn't eaten at all." So the chatter went on, quietly, discreetly, because after all, Saul still had authority from the Chief Priests in Jerusalem to confront all who belonged to The Way.

Finally, the two arrived at the door of a tiny house and without ceremony walked in. Chacham was sitting, as if from time immemorial, in a low chair, a scroll spread out in front of him. He looked up, beaming, and held out his arms to the child.

Ananias remembered how he himself used to run to the old man, climb into his lap, and listen to the gentle words that flowed over and around him. Strangely, he couldn't remember what they were; but he would always go skipping away, his anxieties left behind. And now, it was the same with his nephew. Karmiel would sit for hours, listening to the ancient man drone on and on. And then he would leave, looking as if he had been entrusted with the greatest secret of all.

Ananias set the myrrh and bread on the table, and they all sat down together, pulling off a bite or two and reaching into the deep bowl of red grapes. In the middle of trading neighborhood news, Chacham suddenly leaned forward.

"Ananias. Have you seen Saul? What are you going to do about him?"

The other swallowed his bread hastily and reached for his cup of wine.

"Me?" he said incredulously. "About that evil man? He has blustered and raged; he has caused the imprisonment and death of all he lays his hands on. Can I endanger my family? No! Can I arrest him? Under whose authority?"

Chacham sighed. "He was hit by a bolt of lightning, Ananias, and blinded. That was part of his punishment. I think, in the end, he will suffer as Stephen did, as all the disciples do. No, I don't mean that you should take on that part of God's work, that punishment, into your own hands."

He put one arm around Karmiel as if to shelter him and with the other pointed at the tiny sapling that Chacham had brought. After a moment, he said to the older man, "Look what has happened. A single seed in good soil put there by your hands, your hands that bear the record of all you have done through the years—all the burdens you have carried, all the incense you have burned."

"Give me your hands, my son," he said to Chacham. He pointed to the scars. "You have both rough places, and . . ." He gently turned Chacham's hands up. "And these smooth places. You have shaped and created with fingers that are light in touch. But you also have bumps and lines and bones curved and bent; they are the signatures of your work in the world. Your work . . ." He paused and smiled first at the myrrh sapling and then at the child.

Then he looked piercingly at Ananias, the light in his eyes impossible to ignore. "You have healing hands. Get up and go. Lay them on that blind man and make it possible for him to see the Son."

Chacham leaned back and fell into a brown study.

"It is your choice," the old man murmured, "whether he is to spread the word or not."

Ananias bowed his head and thought of the net he was about to walk into, thought of never seeing his family again, thought of his own choice. Was he a real disciple, or one in name only?

The room was silent, a ray of sun falling on the ancient one as he sat musing as if he were listening to words that only he could hear.

"Come, Karmiel," sighed his uncle. "It is time for us to go." When they had reached the Straight Way, he gave the boy a gentle push in the direction of his own house. Once he was out of sight, Ananias stood a moment in the sunlight, praying for courage.

"Here I am," he said. "Here I am."

Then he turned and walked to the house of Judas, where Saul sat spiritless and sightless, awaiting his knock on the door.

> Lord, grant us the strength and courage to follow your commands so that your spirit may pour through our hands as we reach out to others. Amen.

Acts of Charity:
Peter and the Widows

Peter got up and went with them; and when he arrived, they took him to the room upstairs. All the widows stood beside him, weeping and showing tunics and other clothing that Dorcas had made while she was with them. Peter put all of them outside, and then he knelt down and prayed. He turned to the body and said, "Tabitha, get up." Then she opened her eyes, and seeing Peter, she sat up. (Acts 9:36–43)

She sat in front of the house, rocking gently back and forth on the stool. Above her, the palm trees swayed gently, their shadows brushing the grass at her feet. *At least there is sunlight between the shade,* she thought, and then her grief overcame her.

She wrapped her arms around her swelling waistline as she wept for the man her son would never see. It would be a boy, that she was sure of, and she smiled through her tears, remembering the delight on his face as he entrusted her with his son's care.

"I shall return," he said firmly. "Together, we will found a new generation!" And then he was off to join a group of friends on pilgrimage.

She still saw him in her mind's eye, standing against a blazing sunset, tall and loving and proud.

But she would never see him again. When the messenger brought the news, he knelt in front of her, his face streaked with tears.

The wailing from the upper room grew louder as her mother leaned from the window and called, "Shamira! Shamira! Has he come yet?"

For a moment, she stared agape. "No," her heart cried out. "No, he is gone forever!" She stopped herself just in time. "No one has come," she replied hastily.

Given her swollen ankles and approaching motherhood, climbing the inner stairway to the upper room where the other widows gathered around Tabitha would have been difficult. So she sat by the door as a lookout, ready to let them know when the man they called Peter arrived from Lydda.

But what, after all, could he do? Tabitha had died—Tabitha, who had clothed them with living hope after their husbands had gone to the great beyond. She was the leader of a community of widows—and oh, there were so many. Wars and disputes, sickness, and old age had taken their husbands. And somehow the women they left behind had struggled on, their path made so much smoother by Mother Tabitha, who wove garments for them and taught them beautiful, intricate stitches; who fed them and who gave them a safe place, a small community of their own. When she had first moved here, Tabitha was like her name, a small, vulnerable gazelle, frightened by the least appearance of danger. Then after her husband died, her inner beauty, her generosity, led her to reach out with hand and heart to those in need around her.

Shamira could hear the wailing of the other widows rise and fall like the rhythm of the waves lapping against the shore. She closed her eyes and must have drifted off, because suddenly, there was a hullabaloo around her and a thick-set, muscular man was striding into the house, followed by a crowd. The men in the front looked hopeful and intense, but Shamira could overhear some of the stragglers.

"Who does he think he is? There are no fish here for him to catch," one of them snickered.

His neighbor turned sharply. "He thinks he's the Messiah," he hissed.

A third said with a small smile, "I'll take care of him," and turned away, slipping through the trees.

Shamira shivered at the tone of his voice. She could hear the sound of the widows' footsteps moving down the stairs. The woman in front raised her voice in grieving, and the others joined in, their voices rising and falling as they lamented the life of the one they had loved so much.

As she got up to join the group of women, Shamira saw the visitor shake his head and push through the crowd to the stairwell. One of Peter's companions shouted, "Silence! If you want to help, pray for the Holy Spirit to flow through Peter's fingers!"

Slowly, the room grew still. The women fingered the edges of the shawls Tabitha had woven for them, the deep, rich colors an outpouring of grief and joy together.

And then a voice floated down from above. "Tabitha, get up!"

The women stood stock still, their eyes wide and mouths agape. No one moved or spoke, and in the profound silence, they could hear a soft rustle and a sound of movement.

Suddenly, Peter appeared at the foot of the stairs and threw his arms open to them. "Come up and praise God!" he said joyfully. "He has returned Tabitha to you!"

There was a rush to the stairs. Several of the stragglers frowned, turned on their heels, and pushed out the door. Shamira, whose heart had been in the room with Tabitha from the beginning, stood motionless, weeping with joy.

"She is risen!" she could hear her mother-in-law rejoicing.

As Shamira raised her hands in thanksgiving, the child inside her moved as if he too rejoiced in the coming of new life.

> *God of All Comfort, we are grateful that in the midst of grieving, you offer us hope, and we pray that we may pass that joy on to others by the work of our hands. Amen.*

Angels Among Us: Peter and Rhoda

When he knocked at the outer gate, a maid named Rhoda came to answer. On recognizing Peter's voice, she was so overjoyed that, instead of opening the gate, she ran in and announced that Peter was standing at the gate. They said to her, "You are out of your mind!" But she insisted that it was so. They said, "It is his angel." (Acts 12:13–15)

The young woman pushed back a strand of hair and shifted the heavy wooden tray to one hip. Stealthily, she peered around the edge of the curtain where the men were gathered. They all had their eyes closed, swaying back and forth in the faintly perfumed air. Only three candles were burning, and the room was dark. In the flickering light, she could see they were down on their knees.

A subdued murmur filled the air, and she stood transfixed. Sounds had always fascinated her, ever since she was a child. Her mother had been taken on board a ship by her owners, who were making a pilgrimage to Jerusalem. Months later, they abandoned her, pregnant and dispossessed. It was only by God's grace that another family had rescued her and brought her to Judea, where she gave birth to a daughter.

Rhoda had no idea who her father was, but she imagined him a handsome fisherman, attuned to the ways of the sea. She herself loved the water and dreamed of walking through it, over it, on it; she longed to hear the seabirds calling and feel the cool wash of water on her brow.

She could hear the women in the kitchen making dinner and praying—chop a turnip, say a prayer; peel a potato, pray some more; stir the soup, and softly chant, "May the wishes of our hearts arise up with the fragrance of the meal."

Suddenly, she started. That rapping noise! It sounded just like an old friend of the family knocking at the door. *But it couldn't be*, she said to herself. *He's in prison! That's why they are praying for him* ... and she felt the tears start in her eyes. Tomorrow would be his execution day.

Just then, she noticed John Mark was frowning at her through the curtain's crack. She hurriedly stepped back, and the rapping grew louder. Leaning the tray against the wall, she ran to the door and opened it.

And there he was, knocking at the gate! Her eyes grew wide, and she stood there for a moment, her mouth open.

"It's Peter!" she cried. She turned and ran back, bursting through the curtain into the midst of the praying men.

"It's Peter!" she repeated, and some of the men rose up and angrily came toward her.

"She's mad! Seize her!" they cried.

"No, it's true, he's there. I saw him!"

The babble rose up around her. "She's been drinking! She's possessed! Disturbing a prayer meeting—she ought to be put to the dogs." But John Mark's mother, who had come out from the kitchen, had a gentle heart. "You have seen his angel, little one," she said sadly to Rhoda, "and that means that he is no longer with us."

At that point, the rapping grew louder, more insistent, and Rhoda pulled herself away from the hands that were trying to restrain her and ran out to the gate.

"I really am here," said Peter half-humorously. "And I'm hungry! Let me in!"

Soon he was settled in the middle of the group, happily dipping bread into the stew. "Lock the doors!" said someone. "Blow out the candles—the guards might see us," said another.

"No!" roared Peter with his mouth full. "Let there be light—lots of light! Set the oil burning! The Lord has saved me. He has saved us all!"

And then he stood up, his arms stretched wide, his mantle flowing as if he had wings. The women who had silently gathered in the doorway gasped.

"I was asleep between the guards," Peter began, "and an angel poked me." He laughed aloud. "He poked me! And light poured into the prison. I thought I was dreaming. When I stood up, the chains fell from my body, and even the clanking didn't wake up the guards. So I dressed and put on my sandals, and we walked past two more guards—they were sound asleep! The gate opened by itself—faster than it did here—" and here he winked at Rhoda, who looked down, embarrassed. "Then, the angel left me, and I knew I was awake, so I came to see my old friends."

He sat down again and became the Peter they all knew, dropping crumbs on the floor and spilling his bowl as he turned to talk to someone.

But Rhoda turned away, not knowing whether to laugh or cry. She was no longer the person they all knew. No longer the servant's child turned servant to the family. It was more as if she had become a handmaiden to something infinitely larger.

It was almost as if she herself had seen an angel as if a light had poured on her out of the darkness.

It was almost as if she had been submerged in the waters of the sea and had emerged a new person.

She, after all, had seen someone rise from prison. Peter had returned from the dead.

Light of the World, we pray for the grace to walk out of the prison of the self that we may spread the light of your love to all whom we meet. Amen.

Standing on Two Feet: Paul at Lystra

In Lystra there was a man sitting who could not use his feet and had never walked . . . And Paul, looking at him intently and seeing that he had faith to be healed, said in a loud voice, "Stand upright on your feet." And the man sprang up and began to walk. When the crowds saw what Paul had done, they shouted in the Lycaonian language, "The gods have come down to us in human form!" (Acts 14:8–11)

"**F**ather," the boy said, "they have taken our bull!" He held out his hands in supplication, the breeze rippling the edges of his frayed sleeves.

Irijah, who was repairing a broken well, stopped abruptly and stared speechlessly at his son.

"They came just past noon. The priest was with them. They said the gods had descended,

123

that Zeus and Hermes demanded a sacrifice." The boy's eyes were filled with fear. "They said," and his voice dropped, "if we refused the bull, we would be the ones to go."

In the gloom, Irijah could just make out his wife, standing rigidly in the shadows behind him, clutching the baby. "I dealt with them by myself," Beryl said, a small gleam of pride shining behind the tears ready to fall. "I told Mother to take Mattea into the woods."

"You have done well, my son." Irijah put a hand on his shoulder. So that was the noise he had heard, then––not a joyful one, no bells, no music, just people shouting. "Take them to a safe place now," he commanded. Beryl stood straighter and nodded solemnly, looking like the strong man he was to become.

Irijah turned on his heel and made his way across the field through the gates. As he approached the crowd, he saw a slender, bent figure, leaning on a rod.

"It can't be!" he exclaimed. "Ashur! What happened?"

The man turned slowly, gingerly, as if he was learning where to put his feet. At the sight of his old friend, he threw back his head and laughed. "I can walk!" he shouted. "Look!" and with that, he began a slow dance around Irijah.

"No more sitting at the gate," he said, his eyes filled with awe. "Irijah, they came across the mountain from Iconium and spoke of wonders! They said there is one God, that his Son was sent to help us but was hung from a tree—and then— oh Irijah, I'm so full of joy I can hardly speak. His Son still lives! He came back from the dead! Even Zeus couldn't do that."

"But you've never been able to walk before!" Irijah sputtered.

"The Son can do that too," his friend grinned.

Suddenly, two men ran wildly into the center of the crowd, shouting, "Stop! Stop!"

"That's him," Ashur whispered. "That one. He told me to stand on my own two feet—and I did!"

"Zeus! Zeus! Hermes! Hermes!" the crowd responded, even louder.

Irijah never forgot the scene in front of him. On one side, the temple priest and his helpers, with his own beloved bull between them, horns draped with flowers and leaves. The bull that had fathered so many calves over the years, the one that had given them something to sell in the marketplace, the one that had fed his family. This was the one they were ready to sacrifice.

In front of him, the two men, with anguish on their faces, shouted, "Stop the sacrifice! We are not gods! We are Paul and Barnabas, just humans, like you!"

"Zeus! Zeus! Hermes! Hermes!" the crowd chanted again, and the priest began to push forward toward the temple.

"No!" roared the one they called Hermes, and the crowd quieted. "There's no need to sacrifice—the real living God made everything, the earth and the sea and all that is in them—he doesn't want sacrifice. Just look around you at the gifts he has given you out of his bounty, the gifts that witness to him. You have rains from heaven and a time to grow crops that feed you and your children. Offer up to him your belief, your joy in the world he has given you!"

The crowd began arguing back and forth, and Irijah held his breath and looked hopefully at Ashur. Maybe he would get his bull back after all.

Suddenly, stones began to fly, and the bull reared up, pulling free of the tethers that held him. He stamped and bellowed, then as a stone hit him, turned tail, and ran back through the open gate into the fields. Stones began to fly every which way, many of them landing close to Paul and Barnabas.

"Got him!" someone nearby muttered gleefully as Paul's knees buckled. "Let me try as well," grunted his friend, hoisting back a heavy rock. These were strangers, Irijah saw, but the scene was too chaotic. He turned and ran after his bull, then stopped. The animal was safe, heading home toward the fields he had been raised in.

Suddenly, the crowd turned silent. The two strangers Irijah had overheard were dragging a bundle of clothes—no, it was a person, the one the crowds had called Zeus—out of the gates. They stopped, dusted off their hands, and stood shoulder-to-shoulder.

"He's had it," Irijah heard them say. "We've done our job." They took one more look at the man on the ground, then turned and left.

Irijah and Ashur pushed through the crowd, which had surged forward to see the motionless figure. Suddenly, there was a gasp.

"He lives! He was dead, but he lives!"

Paul sat up shakily, putting his head in his hands. "What happened?" he murmured. "They were stoning me, and then suddenly everything went black. Then, out of nowhere, I heard a voice say, 'Stand on your own two feet,' and—here I am."

He got up unsteadily and brushed himself off.

Ashur bowed and said to Paul, "You have been my staff of life; now I will be yours." He held out his arm, which Paul gratefully took.

Irijah, beckoning to Barnabas, bowed to both of them and smiled. "You may not be gods, but you have saved my bull, my livelihood. Come, let us go home and break bread together."

Dear God, the Rock of our salvation, we pray that we have the strength and the courage to stand on our own two feet so that we may reach out and help others. Amen.

An Eager Listener:
Lydia and the
Washerwoman

A certain woman named Lydia, a worshiper of God, was listening to us; she was from the city of Thyatira and a dealer in purple cloth. The Lord opened her heart to listen eagerly to what was said by Paul. When she and her household were baptized, she urged us, saying, "If you have judged me to be faithful to the Lord, come and stay at my home." And she prevailed upon us. (Acts 16:14–15)

She crept along the riverbank, hardly noticing the pebbles that bruised her feet and the thorny bushes that tore at her clothes. The voices rose and fell, and she desperately wanted to hear what they said. She shifted the heavy basket from one shoulder to another until she could carry it no farther, and it fell heavily, scattering scarlet robes on the rocky shore. The voices were louder now. She had come as close as she dared.

Shaking out the first piece of cloth, Tikvah began to wash it in the river flowing downstream from the gathering. She was small, no taller than the seedling fig she stood next to, and scarcely of an age to be in charge of the household laundry. Yet she was a slave, after all.

She held firmly to the cloth and scrubbed at the stains. She knew what would happen if one of the cloaks vanished in the river, and she winced at the thought. As she dipped the cloth in and out and strained to hear the conversation that flowed with the wind, she vaguely remembered a time when a set of loving arms had held her up to the sun, had dressed and fed her. But that was long ago, and now she was a washerwoman, the lowest shadow in a wealthy household whose gods were made of gold and silver and who were well beyond her understanding.

Day after day, Tikvah came to do the washing and to listen to the women who gathered upstream. These were the ones who chanted beautiful melodious words, who had long silences when the presence of something unknown was so palpable that she could barely resist running to meet it.

Today, though, it was different. A deep voice had suddenly broken in, and the chanting had stopped. She carefully draped the robe over the rock and crept closer.

"Did you send someone to call me?" A man dressed in dusty robes and well-traveled sandals was standing in front of the bewildered women. "We were on our way to Bithynia, but a Macedonian man suddenly appeared and told us to come here. It is the Sabbath, and we are looking for a place of prayer."

The leader stepped forward, a small woman whose piercing eyes and regal bearing commanded attention. "I am Lydia," she said. "And you are standing on sacred ground. We sent for no one. No man has ever joined us here. We are just a group of women," and here she gestured to the others, "doing what women do."

"Which looks like prayer," the man said with a smile and invited her to sit on the rock next to him. "My name is Paul, and I have come to bring you good news, news of a promise made and kept. News that will bring you a new way of life—and it is life forever!"

They crowded around him, and the girl longed to join them. She crept closer, to the edge of the clearing, her eyes so fixed on Paul that she didn't realize that one of his companions had caught sight of her. He deliberately turned his head to contemplate the water, and she came closer.

What she heard left her with an open mouth and a pounding heart. Was it possible, was it actually possible that someone as high as God could really care about these women? About her? She was almost afraid to think about it as if the mere idea would call down thunder and lightning. The only gods she knew were the ones the emperor worshiped, the ones who wanted precious goods—yes, even human beings—as a sacrifice. They were the gods who turned a deaf ear to her pleas for help. And they had no pity when she was whipped—they had no idea how it felt. They were immovable and unknowable.

But this God, this . . . *Christ*, she thought they said! She crept closer, her eyes shining. He had been poor, like her; he had been hurt—oh so badly—and he still lived! He understood what it was like to toil and to hunger, to be beaten, and to be betrayed.

"Yes!" said Lydia, suddenly springing up. "We will all be baptized—every one of us! And you and your men are welcome at my house. Come! What are we waiting for?" She followed Paul to the river, the other women close behind.

Timothy, the one who had caught sight of the small figure trembling on the edge, turned his head and smiled gently at her. "You have made the right choice," he said quietly. "Come with us."

So she too was baptized in the river. As the others gathered up their belongings and set out to return to the city, she quietly faded into the brush and sat near her basket of laundry.

Nothing had changed. She still had to wash the clothes and carry them back to the house. If anything, her path was more difficult. Knowing the truth, she had to go back among those who worshiped statues that meant nothing.

Yet, everything had changed. Someone was listening; someone had heard her. She felt as if someone were holding her in the palm of his hand.

She picked up her basket and followed in the Son's footsteps, walking resolutely back up the hill, her path crossed by the shadows of the tall wooden fence that surrounded the house. As she opened the door and shifted the burden of the laundry to her other shoulder, she looked back. The sun gleamed on the treetops, lighting the path she had taken. Silently Tikvah repeated what she remembered hearing Lydia say: "If you have judged me to be faithful, Lord, come and stay at my home." And then she went in.

O Lord of the oppressed, we pray that we may follow the path you have set for us, even as we are burdened by the toils and troubles of the day. Amen.

Eutychus Finds the Way

On the first day of the week, when we met to break bread, Paul was holding a discussion with them; since he intended to leave the next day, he continued speaking until midnight. There were many lamps in the room upstairs where we were meeting. A young man named Eutychus, who was sitting in the window, began to sink off into a deep sleep while Paul talked still longer. Overcome by sleep, he fell to the ground three floors below and was picked up dead. But Paul went down, and bending over him took him in his arms, and said, "Do not be alarmed, for his life is in him." (Acts 20:7–12)

Ariella laid her head against the door, a long black scarf hiding her greying hair. Despite the heat, she pulled it close around her shoulders. It had sheltered her mother when the baby, her only sister, had died; and

135

again, when her father died. Her husband had long passed into the great beyond, but through the thin weavings, she could still feel his warm arms around her and hear his gruff voice grow soft.

She jerked back, realizing she was getting sleepy, and peered into the room, careful not to call attention to herself. Other women were waiting in the hall with her, ready to serve dinner to the guest, who had not long before landed on the shore. Inside, the air was getting stuffy, and she could see dust swirling about the oil lamps on the floor. They cast a flickering light on the roomful of men, all sitting in a half-circle around the one they called Paul. The fragrance of lamb and spices wafted down the hall, almost hiding the musky scent of the robes of those who had come directly from the ship.

Her son was there in back of the crowd, and she saw him rise quietly and make his way to a window. *He must be hot*, she thought. They were all gathered in the top floor of the storehouse, where no one could reach them until they unfurled the rope ladder. Her son settled himself on the sill, and she was happy to see he looked alert and interested. It hadn't always been so. Of all her children, he was the one she cherished, despite his illness. And illness it was, something that even Cybele, on the top of Mt. Ida, couldn't cure.

Every so often, he would suddenly drop off to sleep, and it was as if he were dead. He was breathing, yes, but there was no way to wake him. Then, he would suddenly sit up with a startled expression and continue whatever he had been saying or doing. He had no memory of those bouts, those fits, as she thought of them. She had climbed the mountain with offerings of beautiful figs she had picked herself. She had gone from altar to altar, pleading for him. He was bright and funny, and she so much wanted to find him a bride, but that apparently was not to be. So she followed him from place to place, making sure that he was awake when he needed to be. It was not the life for a young man, she knew that; but she also knew he needed protection.

She sighed and tried to understand what Paul was saying. He was speaking about following the Way . . . didn't she already do that, with her offerings and prayers on the mountain? But this way seemed to be different. She listened more closely. Jesus—there was something about Jesus—a young man who loved his God, loved everyone so much that he went willingly to the cross. Looking at her son, she could understand that kind of love. *Maybe Jesus would have loved me, too*, she thought, and tears filled her eyes as she pictured of the young man's mother, standing by his feet at the cross, torn with grief.

Paul went on, and she lost the thread of what he was saying. Suddenly, there was a movement at the window. Her son had reached over and unlatched the blinds, and a slight breeze stirred in the room. He breathed deeply, and his head fell forward and he began swaying from side to side. She rose in terror, her throat so tight she could barely cry his name.

Paul stopped in mid-sentence, and the man next to Eutychus tried to grab his arm, but too late. The blinds swung open and Eutychus disappeared. There was a loud thump.

"Get the ladder!" someone shouted, and a young man impetuously swung himself over the window and tried to climb down the face of the building. "Come back! Don't be foolish!" The chorus of voices grew louder and louder as the ladder was unfurled and one by one, they climbed down to where a slender body lay flat on his back.

Ariella pushed her way through the crowd and gathering her skirts, made her way down to the ground. She fell on her knees by her son. His face was as white as the bread she had made this morning and he was still—so still. He wasn't breathing. The sound of her wailing rose above the clamor of the crowd.

"Make way!" cried a deep voice, and all fell silent as Paul approached. He knelt by Eutychus's side, laid his hands on his chest, and spoke softly.

Then he stretched himself upon the young man three times, and said, "O Lord my God, I pray, let this man's soul come into him again."

Eutychus blinked and sat up. At that, Paul quietly turned and slowly climbed back up the ladder. Almost everyone followed him except Ariella and those who had been near Eutychus when he fell.

"Mother!" he said, and Ariella thought that was the most beautiful word she had ever heard. "Was I dreaming? I thought I heard someone say, 'Go forth on the Way, my Son.'" He shook his head, and she stared at him in wonder. She hadn't heard Paul say that.

"'Go forth on the Way.' Where is the man who was with me? I must see him! I need to know more!" And Eutychus rose to his feet and ran nimbly up the ladder, vanishing into the room, where Paul was speaking.

Well after midnight, Eutychus shook her awake and told her the news. He had decided that for him, following the Way meant going with Paul as he traveled. She was up the rest of the night, packing his bag with clothes and food and wiping away her tears. *It was a miracle*, she thought. It was both more glorious and more wrenching than the healing she had prayed for on the mountain. But it was real. Her son had woken up in more ways than one, she thought, as she looked at his bright eyes and eager expression.

Ariella sighed. It would be all right, she thought. He seemed to have a kind of protection that even she had been unable to give.

As he left the next morning, she clenched her hands around his farewell gift—a cross made from a piece of the ladder's rope. Perhaps the One who spoke to him, who called him "Son," would be revealed. Perhaps when he reached the end of his journey, Eutychus would reappear at her door, rejoicing in a new life.

Her own Way was clear. She would remain in her own house, a living testimony to his healing.

> Lord, you have set us all on the path of our life. Give us the grace to hear your voice and to follow you wherever you lead. Amen.

The Viper Meets its Match: Sea-Going with Paul

After we had reached safety, we then learned that the island was called Malta. The natives showed us unusual kindness. Since it had begun to rain and was cold, they kindled a fire and welcomed all of us around it. Paul had gathered a bundle of brushwood and was putting it on the fire, when a viper, driven out by the heat, fastened itself on his hand. When the natives saw the creature hanging from his hand, they said to one another, "This man must be a murderer; though he has escaped from the sea, justice has not allowed him to live." He, however, shook off the creature into the fire and suffered no harm. (Acts 28:1–5)

The wind was blowing so hard that the young man braced himself against a tree trunk. He often came to this promontory; it was a good place to reconnect with what he loved best—the sea. He closed his eyes and savored the feel of raindrops on his face. *It must be like standing on the prow of a ship*, he thought, with the ocean spray parting in front of you like a path to the unknown. Oh, how he longed to go to sea! He could hear the waves crashing against the shore.

No, he thought, opening his eyes, *that wasn't the waves*. He clambered down the hillock and sprinted toward the reef where a ship was being battered against the stones. Its hull was splintered, and people were jumping wildly into the water. Off to his left, wreckage had washed ashore. One piece that landed higher up on the shore seemed to be moving. It was alive!

He dashed to where the sailor lay, exhausted and barely breathing. The boy turned him over and pounded on his back. Water poured from the man's throat. Finally, he lay shivering, eyes closed.

"Come, friend," the boy said, "let's find you shelter." He leaned down and hoisted him over his shoulder. "Hang on," he said, and walked slowly to where the crowd had gathered.

Bedraggled sailors were everywhere, clothing torn and dripping, moaning in pain as they tried to straighten a leg or bend an arm. Others just sat, looking dazed. The townspeople had rushed to the scene, bringing blankets and food. His brothers were struggling to carry a big pot, while his mother scolded them to be careful. "The soup is hot!" she said. "I spent all morning making it. Don't spill it!"

The man he had carried tugged at his cloak. "You can put me down." Once on the ground, he tried to speak, his voice rough from the saltwater. "Thank you," he croaked, and smiled weakly. "I'm Melech. What's your name?"

"Zunzana." The man looked puzzled. "It means 'bumblebee,'" the boy explained. "This is Malta, the island of honey. My parents are beekeepers."

The man gave him a piercing look. "No," he said. "You are Dominic. You saved my life. In my country, that name means 'of the Lord.'"

The boy shook his head. "Lord?" he asked. "Who is that?"

Melech looked at him in astonishment, but before he could answer, a short, bearded man, bow-legged and limping, passed near them, carrying a pile of brush. "We'll have a fire soon," said the boy, comfortingly. "And then you'll eat my mother's soup. She's—" He never finished his sentence, because his eye caught movement in the brush.

He jumped up, but he was too late. At that moment, the viper leaped out and sank its fangs into the man's hand.

He roared in pain and with a mighty shake of his arm flung the viper far over the sand into the sea. The whole crowd grew still. The man bowed his head, held his hand up to the sky, and after a minute, soberly continued to build the fire.

The murmurs rose.

"He'll die."

"It's a viper. No one can survive that."

The crowd grew more and more restive.

"Oh no. Paul!" Melech murmured and hid his face in his hands.

The man called Paul quietly looked around, reached for a bowl, and started dipping soup to hand to the sailors. No one offered to help, and the boy felt ashamed. Here was someone about to die, yet he was concerned only about the well-being of others.

When he stood up to lend a hand, his father put out an arm to stop him. "He's bedeviled," he hissed. "The viper bite proves it. That's the criminal the ship was carrying."

Paul continued calmly to serve the others, and only sat down when everyone else had his fill. By then, the murmurs had gotten louder.

"He's a demon!"

"No, he's a god! See, he withstood the serpent's bite."

"That's because of his wizardry," said one.

"It's because he's a good man," countered another.

This went on and on as the sun began to sink. In the meantime, Paul finished his meal and set about helping to gather up the sailors' belongings. Many of them, having both food and rest, got up and worked with him.

Suddenly, there was a shout. Over the hill appeared a small procession, the leader Publius at the head. By the time he reached Paul, the crowd was staring in awe. No one on the island had ever survived a viper's bite; and yet there was Paul, talking calmly to the greatest man on the island.

Suddenly, without warning, Publius went down on his knees before Paul.

"He's a God!" the crowd shouted. "He killed the viper!"

But Dominic shook his head. *No*, he thought, *he's a man. But what a man!*

Later that day he learned Paul had healed Publius's father. *So that's what "Lord" means*, he thought. *And Dominic is my new name.* He shook his head in wonderment. As the days passed, he watched Paul pray and lay hands on the tired and lame, the sick and the grieving, and saw them walk away with glory on their faces. *They have a new life. That's who he is*, the boy thought.

But it wasn't until he himself had been dipped bodily into the sea by Paul's hands, baptized in the name of the Lord, that he felt he had truly become Dominic.

Several months later, he stood by Melech's side on the ship pulling away from shore, brushing tears from his eyes as he saw his parents for the last time. Then, as he turned to face the sea, the rising sun lit his hair with fire and his heart with searing joy.

I am following the path, Dominic thought. *I am walking on water to meet my Lord.* And he lifted his hands to the heavens very much as Paul had done.

> *Merciful Lord, we are grateful that you have called us to follow you both on land and on sea. We ask that you help us see the dangers and distractions in our own lives so that we may be open to learning from the words and lives of your apostles. Amen.*

Glossary of Names

Adriel: *God's helper*
Adva: *Small wave or ripple*
Ami: *Trustworthy, reliable*
Amidan: *My people are righteous*
Ananias: *The Lord is gracious*
Ariella: *Light or altar of God*
Aryeh: *Lion*
Ashur: *One who is happy, who walks*
Avar Araphel: *To pass through darkness*
Barnabas: *Son of encouragement or consolation*
Barsabbas: *Son of the Father*
Beryl: *Bear*
Casiphia: *Money, silver*
Chacham: *Student of sages*
Chayim: *Life*
Dominic: *Of the Lord*
Eema: *Mother*
Eliana: *My God has answered*
Elrad: *God rules*

Enge, benge, stupe, stenge: *Eeny meeny, miny, mo (from Sholem Aleichem's rhyme about counting)*
Eutychus: *Fortunate*
Irijah: *The fear of the Lord*
John Mark: *Yahweh is gracious; polite, shining*
Joseph: *He will add; increase*
Judas: *The praise of the Lord; confession*
Justus: *Upright, just*
Karmiel: *God's vineyard*
Kenut: *Honesty*
Lazarus: *My God has helped (from the Hebrew "Eleazar")*
Lydia: *Beautiful; worshiper of God*
Maoz: *Fortress; strength*
Martha: *Lady; mistress*
Mary: *Beloved; bitterness*
Mattea: *God's gift*
Matthias: *Gift of Yahweh*
Melech: *King; counselor*
Miriam: *Rebellion*
Mordecai: *Warrior*
Myyeh: *Myrrh*
Nicodemus: *The victory of the people*
Nuriel: *Light of God; fire of God*
Omri: *Servant*
Paul: *Small; humble*
Peter: *A rock or stone*

Publius: *Of the people*
Reuven: *"Look, a son"*
Rhoda: *Rose*
Saul: *Asked or prayed for*
Sapphira: *Gem or jewel*
Shamira: *Guardian*
Shiprah: *Beautiful*
Stephen: *Crowned*
Tabitha: *Clear-sighted; a gazelle*
Thomas: *Twin*
Tikvah: *Faith; hope*
Timothy: *Honoring God*
Yaiyr: *Whom God enlightens*
Yirmaya: *God is exalted*
Yiskah: *To gaze*
Zaccheus: *Clean; pure*
Zunzana: *Bumblebee*

Bibliography

Campbell, Mike. "Behind the Name: The Etymology and History of First Names." https://www.behindthename.com.

Halseth, Joern Andre. *Hitchcock's Bible Names Dictionary*. Truthbetold Ministry, 2017. Google Books. https://books.google.com/books?id=yaWUDwAAQBAJ.

"Jewish English Lexicon." https://jel.jewish–languages.org.

Potts, Cyrus A. *Dictionary of Bible Proper Names*. New York: Abington Press, 1922.

"The Prayer of St. Francis." *The Book of Common Prayer*. New York: Abington Press, 1979.

Smith, Stelman, and Judson Cornwall. *The Exhaustive Dictionary of Bible Names*. Newberry, FL; Bridge Logos Foundation, 1998.

About the Author

Patricia Marks, retired English professor and Episcopal deacon, is following her childhood dream of writing. She has published over seventy academic articles and reviews, as well as five books. Much of her research has focused on nineteenth-century satire and caricature. She continues to enjoy researching, writing, and publishing, and has expanded her scope to include meditations, Bible stories, and poetry.

A graduate of Douglass College, she received her Ph.D. from Michigan State University and taught in the English Department at Valdosta State University for thirty years. During her career she received many fellowships, grants, and honors, among them the Regents' Distinguished Professorship for Teaching and Learning, the Governor's Award in the Humanities, and National Endowment and Mellon Foundation fellowships. She has served as a reader for a number of publications, including *Victorian Periodicals Review* and *American Periodicals*, and is on the editorial board of *Studies in American Culture*. A retired Episcopal deacon in the Diocese of Georgia at Christ Church, Valdosta, she remains active in church outreach and community organizations, giving book reviews and teaching classes for Learning in Retirement. Along with her astrophysicist husband Dennis, she takes delight in adventurous travel.

Printed in the United States
By Bookmasters